SUSAN HILL

In the
Springtime
of the Year

VINTAGE BOOKS
London

Published by Vintage 2012

8 10 9 7

Copyright © Susan Hill 1974, 2008

Susan Hill has asserted her right under the Copyright, Designs
and Patents Act 1988 to be identified as the author of this work

First published in Great Britain in 1974 by Hamish Hamilton
First published in paperback in 1976 by Penguin Books

Vintage
Random House, 20 Vauxhall Bridge Road,
London SW1V 2SA

www.vintage-books.co.uk

Addresses for companies within The Random House Group Limited
can be found at: www.randomhouse.co.uk/offices.htm

The Random House Group Limited Reg. No. 954009

A CIP catalogue record for this book
is available from the British Library

ISBN 9780099570486

Penguin Random House is committed to a sustainable future for
our business, our readers and our planet. This book is made from
Forest Stewardship Council® certified paper.

Printed and bound in Great Britain by Clays Ltd, St Ives plc

In happy memory of David

PART ONE

1

She closed the door behind her, and then it was quite silent, quite dark. She stood, and she could smell very faintly the dry smell of the bracken, coming over the common. Everything was dry now, for three weeks the sun had shone. It tired her. But throughout April and May, it had rained, and that, too, had been tiring, the endless, dull pattering on to the cottage roof. She had not expected to notice, certainly not to be disturbed by, those things – weather, heat or damp or cloud, night or day, things which existed outside her own self, her own misery. But they had been like burns or abrasions that never healed, irritating her, intruding.

She waited until she could see just a little, and then go down the narrow path between the vegetable beds, and beyond the fruit trees, to where the hens were. There was no sound tonight from the owls in the copse, over to the left of the cottage, no stirring in the trees themselves.

She thought suddenly, I am alone. I am entirely alone on this earth; there are no other people, no animals or birds or insects, no breaths or heartbeats, there is no growing, the leaves do not move and the grass is dry. There is nothing.

And this was a new feeling. No, not a feeling. Loneliness was a feeling, and fear of the empty house and of the long days and nights, and the helpless separation from Ben – feelings. This was different. A condition. A fact. Simply, being absolutely alone.

Then, a cloud slid off the face of the moon, and there was a little light, she could see the grey trunks of the old fruit trees and the bunched tops of the elms. There was no colour, but there were shapes. She began to walk slowly down the garden. It was only nine o'clock. It was the end of August. Each night now, she would put the hens into their coop a few minutes earlier, and those minutes would bring the winter forward. She did not want to think of winter.

When the donkey brayed from the meadow, she stopped in terror, startled out of herself, almost out of her own body, by the suddenness of it, and by the sadness, too, for it had always seemed to her something sad, and painful, this cry, like a harsh appeal for help, comfort – though Ben had laughed at her, the donkey was perfectly happy now, he said, how could it not be, with an acre of meadow, and the affection they both gave it. And Ben's brother Jo had told her about animals in Africa, hyenas and zebras and jackals, which made even more weird noises though he had only read about them in books, only imagined the sounds. There was so much Jo had told her, so much that he knew, partly from reading, partly from some mixture of awareness and intuition within him, about the world. And Jo's ears were sharper than anyone's, he could tell every bird cry, and their different noises from season to season, he could distinguish the movements of a rabbit, a fox or a stoat, hidden in the undergrowth. Jo. It was a week, more than a week, since Jo had been; she did not lose track of time so easily now, as in those first weeks, when morning and night, Monday and Friday and all the hours between them had been shuffled together, and with no purpose to any of them.

The donkey brayed again, hearing her, and she called back to it softly, no longer startled. Why had Ben bought a donkey? Leading it home, with a soft rope tied around its ulcerated neck, a present for her, and for himself, too, he had said, something living, to belong to them. He had found it tied up with a great leather collar and chain, to a tree by the roadside beyond Long Thicket, and owned by a tinker who was glad enough to sell it, for a pound, and the cheese, boiled eggs and beer that Ben had with him in his bag.

The animal had looked at them out of dead eyes that day, and its coat was scabbed and dull, it had shuffled down the path into the meadow, and then stood, only stood, unaware of its new freedom from the collar and chain, and perhaps afraid of it, also, afraid of the great expanse of grass.

For days it had stood like that, close up to the fence,

and when Ruth had taken down water or hay, it had not touched them; then, after a few days, had bent its head to the bucket only when she had gone out of sight, back into the cottage. It had taken weeks, weeks of patience and gentleness, of speaking to the animal as she came down the path, of daring to put her hand, for a second or two, on the coarse, sore neck.

At the beginning, they had given no name to it; Ben had gone down the garden and only called out 'Here, donkey', or 'Boy'. It was Jo who had said 'Balaam' and gone and found the Bible and the story of Balaam's ass, which saw an angel and spoke to it in a human voice. Ben had said no, Balaam was the man, his donkey had not had a name. But then, they had all of them looked down towards the meadow and seen the animal shambling off a little distance from the fence, head up, ears pricked forward, beginning to explore, and at once it had seemed right, the only possible name. Balaam. Though Dora Bryce had sneered at them when she heard it, and her husband said it was blasphemy, Ruth was unsurprised, for she was used to all that, had accepted from the beginning that they did not like her, and would never forgive her for marrying Ben. Jo had said at once that the donkey's name was his idea – Jo, honest and fierce in Ruth's defence, Jo, the youngest, the cleverest one. But it had made no difference. Nothing would ever make any difference.

There had been days, during these months since the spring, when she had thought of letting the donkey go, selling it. After Ben's death, she had paid no attention to it, only stared, as she had stared at everything else, without interest, as it lumbered about the meadow, grazing. It had missed her, missed the attention it had grown used to in its new life here, there had been mornings when it had come up to the fence and peered towards the house, lifted up its head and brayed. When Jo came to see her, which had been almost every day, he would go down to the meadow, refill the water bucket, talk to the animal, so that it did not feel, as Ruth felt, completely bereft, completely alone.

Now, as she heard it down in the darkness ahead, she thought again, should I keep it? Why do I keep it? And knew why – because it was hers, and Ben had bought it, it was part of the old life, and now she no longer wanted everything which reminded her of that to be done away with. Besides, she liked the donkey, liked to see its ungainly grey body and odd legs, it comforted her, as the hens were a comfort, she would not like to look down towards the meadow and see it empty now.

The apple trees grew so close together, the path between them was so narrow that always, at night, she put a hand out in front of her, feeling her way like someone blind, to ward off the down-hanging branches. Now, as she reached out, she tripped off the edge of the tussocky grass path on to the soil, and half-fell forwards, against the trunk of a tree. She was not hurt. She righted herself, and moved the palms of her hands up and down over the bark. It was scabbed and grainy in patches, and very cold. Ben had been going to fell the apple trees. They were years old and neglected: Old Slye, who had owned the cottage for half a century, before them, had never pruned them, so that now, there were only a very few apples each year, hard and small and bitter, growing in clumps at the very top. Cut them down, Ben had said, and we'll have firewood enough for years – for apple wood was good, it burned sweetly and left a soft, clean ash. Then he would plant saplings, more apple and pear, too, and a quince, and meanwhile, until they grew up, there would be an open view, straight down from the cottage to the meadow and the beech woods beyond.

Now, the trees would stay. For even if one of the local men had been willing to fell them for her, she would never ask. She asked nothing of anyone, had vowed not to do so, the first day. Besides, the trees, like Balaam, were part of the old life, of everything she now wanted to cling to.

She realised after a few moments of standing there, touching the tree, that she no longer felt strange, the only person in an empty, dead world. The donkey had brayed, she could smell the last of the sweet stocks and the tobacco plants, and there were the hens, just ahead of her, in a line on the top of the coop. Other things lived. The world turned.

The pleasure she took in caring for the hens was the only thing that had never left her, and she had clung to that. This nightly journey down the garden had been one thing, the only thing, to which she looked forward each day. The hens knew her. They were trusting. And reliable themselves, too, always in their places as darkness fell, ready to be put away. They made small noises which seemed to come from deep within their plumage, dove-like sounds, as they heard her lift the latch of the gate into their run. She put her hands round each one firmly, and felt the softness of feather, and the sinewy wings, and, coming through them, the blood-and-flesh warmth. They never struggled, unless she picked one of them up awkwardly, and then it would beat its wings into her face, and she had to go on to the next, wait for that one to settle down again.

Ben had laughed at her care for the hens. He had no dislike of them, they were useful, he said, and no trouble, they gave good eggs. But they were stupid creatures, weren't they, with such small heads, small brains, they made such graceless darts and bobs of movement. He would never believe that Ruth could tell one from another, to him they all looked the same, dull russet-coloured. Balaam now, Balaam he could take an interest in, the donkey amused him, and it had character, but what character had the hens? Ruth had only shaken her head, unable to explain, and he had not minded, as she did not mind his teasing of her.

She shut down the flap of the coop and bolted it, and listened for a moment to the scuttling sounds inside, as the birds settled themselves for the night.

But in the end they went quiet, and then it was over, and there was nothing else to do except walk back up to the cottage, and she did not want to do it, she never wanted to go back. Not because she was afraid. Or else, if afraid, then only of her own feelings and memories and of the silence that pressed in on her ears within every room, of the sound of her own movements.

She lingered outside. She went to the vegetable patch and knelt down, touching the cold, damp leaves of the spinach plants, and burying her hands deep into the soil, feeling about until she found a potato, and then another; she would cook them, perhaps, make up a small fire and bake them and eat them with butter, it would be a treat. It would be something.

The scarlet runner-bean flowers were grey like laburnum pods in the moonlight. It had been Jo who had come up, and planted and staked them, Jo who had drilled the seed rows, and then thinned out the plants as they grew up. Jo, never asking, only seeing what needed to be done, and getting on with it in silence, keeping things going. Jo knew that he was the only person she would allow at the cottage, to help her, and sometimes to talk. Jo, Ben's brother and so different from Ben, different from them all. He was fourteen and he might have been a hundred years old, he knew so much, had so much wisdom, so much awareness of himself and of others. She had been able to bear it most easily because he did not look like Ben either, though even with fourteen years between them the brothers had been very close. But she loved Jo for himself for what he was, for how he treated her, not because he was a Bryce and her dead husband's brother.

*

In the kitchen, she said, 'I will cook them. The potatoes I will cook them,' and she had spoken, almost cried the words aloud. It no longer terrified her, that she talked to herself, she no longer thought that it was a sign of madness.

During the first weeks, she had gone up and down the stairs, stood in the middle of this room or that, she did not know where, and talked; about what had happened, and how, about her own thoughts and feelings and what she would do. She had talked to Ben, too, because he was still there, wasn't he, just behind her shoulder, at the end of the landing, on the other side of a door, and it was sometimes just ordinary talk, she might only say, 'Hello, Ben.' But for the rest of the time, she blamed him, screamed out in resentment 'Where are you? Where are you? Why did you have to die? Oh, why did you die?'

What she would not do was talk to anyone else except, occasionally, to Jo. She had been silent, unless when answering what questions she must about the immediate arrangements, or else refusing something they wanted to give her, food or drink or comfort. They had all watched her, they had been anxious, clucked advice at her, admonished, warned. But she had not talked, or wept, in front of any of them.

'*I will cook them.*'

The potatoes lay in her hand, heavy as eggs, dusty. But she would have to kindle a fire, and she could not make that effort, just for herself, for cooking two potatoes. The range was out. Jo was the one who came up to light it, when he thought that she might need the water hot, and Jo had cooked things for her once or twice, too, until he saw that she did not want them.

But since July, and the long hot days of sun, she had let the range go out, and left it. She washed every day, and her hair, as well, in cold water, and she ate at odd times, in the middle of the morning, or late at night, bits of fruit and cheese or raw vegetables, and the last side of baked ham, never sitting down, with knife and fork and plate, just wandering about the empty house and garden. The eggs she sold now, all of them, she needed the money.

People had sent food up to her at first – even Dora Bryce, who hated her for her independence; plate-pies and legs of chicken, cakes, loaves of bread. She did not eat them. She resented their gifts, saw them as an imposition upon her, though now, she was ashamed of herself, at this churlish rejection of what had only been kindness, after all, and caring. She had not known that it was in her nature to be like that, but her nature had changed, hadn't it? Or else the truth of it had been uncovered by Ben's death.

Once, though, she had tried to cook, just once. Jo had come in the morning with a rabbit, ready skinned and cut up, though he had said nothing about it, only found a dish and left it there, on a slab in the larder. And that night, she had found fat and flour and made a pie, with a sauce of stock and herbs and onions for the meat, and the smell of the baking filled the house like new life, her stomach had felt hollow with longing for the food, it had made a pain below her ribs.

The pie had come out of the oven with a soft, barley-brown crust, the meat and gravy spilling out, dark as port, over the white plate. Yet, when she had put a forkful of it into her mouth, her throat had gagged and she could not swallow, she held the meat against her tongue until it went cold, lumpy, and she had rushed outside to be sick upon the grass.

The pie had stayed there, congealing, losing its glaze and savour until, after a couple of days, the flies settled on to it, and she threw it all into the swill bin, which Carter came and emptied every week, for his pigs.

Ruth had wept, then, out of shame and guilt at the waste of the food, and for pity of the rabbit, which had been living, and then shot dead, and all to no purpose.

After that, there had been no more cooking.

She left the potatoes on the kitchen table, and drank a cup of cold milk. And all the time it was there, lying at the back of her mind like a dog, waiting to leap out and attack, the thought of what she must do. For the past fortnight, now, she had half-acknowledged that it was there, only to draw herself back from it in dread. When she imagined all that it would mean, her heart pounded, she had to clutch on to a chair or the wall to steady herself. She dare not do it, go there, find him, and ask the questions, listen, discover. For, once she had discovered, none of it could ever again be forgotten.

The pile of sewing, sent down by Mrs. Rydal, lay beside her chair. They were always small, fussy jobs, tedious and unrewarding, jobs no one else would do. She would have liked the chance to make something new, a dress or some petticoats, but even if they felt she could manage it now, they would not ask her; she was the girl who did the mending not the making.

It did not engross her, and so she went over and over the same things in her mind, while her hands patched the elbows of shirts and darned socks, shortened or lengthened hems. Much of the time, it seemed to her that the garments were only fit to be thrown away, the material was almost past repairing. Yet the Rydals owned half the villages and woods for miles around, they could not be poor. It was poor people who darned and redarned, and made up a sheet out of two old ones, sides to middle. If she had had the choice, she would have refused the work, but she had to live, and the only other way to make money would have been to sell the cottage. It was hers, bought with the money Godmother Fry had left her, they had been proud, she and Ben both, that they were not tenants.

Leaving here she could not contemplate because it was all she had left to cling to, it was Ben, it was life to her, familiar. She dreaded change, new places. And so, she did the sewing, and ironing, too. One of the men brought parcels over from Ridge Farm, and she herself walked back with them and, as often as not, tried to leave them somewhere, to slip into the kitchen when it was empty, and leave again at once, to avoid meeting anyone, having to talk.

People around here were lucky, they said, to have Rydal for an employer or a landlord, he paid good enough wages and kept the houses in repair – though he worked the men hard. Ben had worked hard, but that had only been his nature, he had hated to be idle, could never rest, even at home in the evenings, though he had been up and out at half past six, and not home again until seven – or later, in the summer.

'Sit down,' she had said sometimes, 'just sit down with me.' And he would do so, to please her, but after a few moments, he was restless, he would lean over and start to fiddle with the fire, re-arranging the logs, getting up a draught, and then remember some job to be done. Well, she had not minded. It was the way he was. And he had been there, hadn't he, there with her, even when he was digging in the garden or mending the roof of the shed, she had been able to hear him, to catch sight of him from the window. He had been there.

She looked down at the clothes. A jacket with the collar frayed, a skirt missing two buttons. Nothing.

The room had gone cooler. The lamp threw its shadows. And if she did not begin to work now, did not find her needle and thread, she would just sit for hours, until she was tired enough to go to bed, sit without moving, her hands in her lap, staring ahead. It seemed now that not just half a year, but half of her life had gone by like that – except that it was not life, it was not anything, except time passing, and the thoughts which passed to and fro like shuttles, the same pictures she saw in her mind, the same words remembered.

She began to sew. She said, I am getting better, and I am doing it by myself for that was the most vital thing of all, if she was going to recover somehow, she should do it without help. Though there were days when she did not believe that anything had changed after all, days which were worse than those at the beginning, because she was no longer shocked or numb now, and so she knew, that it was true and would go on being true, and it was on those days that, if she had not been so afraid, she would have killed herself. It was what they were all expecting, wasn't it? Perhaps even what they wanted – Ben's family, and all those people whose help she had spurned.

'Burying herself up there. Brooding. Living from hand to mouth. Is she right in her mind? A young woman, twenty-one years old just, and alone in that cottage, talking to herself, never giving thought for anyone else.'

Perhaps they thought that she was becoming like old man Moony, out in his hovel beyond Priors Fen. But no, that was different, for he had been odd since anyone could remember, a cussed, dirty old man, who stumped for hours about the countryside, eyes down, giving no one Good-day. They accepted Moony. There had always been one like him, somewhere about. Moony had come back from the war and some said that was what had crazed him, that was the reason for his shutting himself away and trusting no one.

Was that how she wanted to be? 'Proud,' they said, 'she was always proud.' And it was more than likely she didn't wash or bother with herself now, didn't clean the house – though Jo told them that was not true. She had kept herself and the house as tidy and fresh as she had always done. That was what her pride meant.

So they talked about her, Dora Bryce, and Alice, and the wives and mothers of the men Ben had worked with, and told anyone who passed through the village too. They waited for her to go mad and run about the countryside stark naked, to be taken away. To be found dead.

No one missed anything. They knew how often she went across the four fields and down through the slopes of the beech woods to Helm Bottom, and how long she stayed there, crouched near to where the tree had fallen; they knew that she went up, and how often, not by day but at night, to the graveyard. There was nothing they did not know, and although she shut her doors and bolted her windows and the elms were thick and the bracken grew high as a man, although it was a mile to the next house and three to the village, she felt that they could see every movement she made, listen to her voice and her crying.

She sat on, sewing, and the house was quiet as a coffin and outside, too, it was quite still and the trunks of the beeches were like columns of lead under the moon.

In his bed, at the top of the house in Foss Lane, Jo lay, his eyes open, so that he saw the thin band of night sky, where the curtains did not meet together, and thought of Ruth, as he always thought of her, with love and fear. He knew that whatever she needed, it could only come from him, all the responsibility for her had fallen from his brother's shoulders on to his own, and he was not always sure how well he could bear it, along with his own grief, which he had to keep locked within him, he dreaded that he might one day let Ruth down, and be unable to help it. She said, 'I manage. I don't need anyone,' and only he knew that it was not true.

He felt tired. Yet, in the end, there was always something, a hard core of energy and hope which he could touch like a charm, and draw strength from. If he feared, he did not ever despair. He was master of himself.

Sounds carried. A squirrel or some night-bird scuttling over the tin roof of the shed at the other side of the garden, might have been scuttling in her own head. She folded the pillow case, and put needle and thread and thimble back into the padded work-box. She went upstairs to bed, and her arms and legs felt as if they were held down by weights. She would sleep, as she always did now, a sleep that was dark and thick and stifling, as though it was she who had the great clods of soil and turf piled on top of her. She did not dream or stir, nor ever want to waken, and have another day begin.

But tonight, after only an hour, she opened her eyes suddenly, and heard the silence in the house, and beyond it, and remembered what she had to do. It was time, it was six months since Ben had died, and now, she had to know about that death, every detail, to discover all the things she had shut out, by pressing her hands over her ears and screaming, so that they would not make her listen. Well, they had not. In the end, they had gone away. She knew nothing except that a tree had fallen in Helm Bottom, and Ben was dead.

Potter, the man who had been with him, lived a mile away, across the common. Tomorrow, she would go there. Tomorrow.

She slept again.

PART TWO

2

The day before, she had been into the market at
Thefton and bought a present for Ben there, a small,
rough chunk of rose quartz crystal, from the one-eared
man who set up his stall with jewellery and china ornaments, bits of this and that picked up from houses
around the country. There was always something new
and strange, she loved to stand, looking, imagining
where things had come from and the people they had
once belonged to, though she had never bought before.

The stone was grey and pitted on the underside, like
a piece of lava, but where it had been cut, the quartz
glittered like chips of ice flushed through with pink, in
the sunlight. And suddenly, standing there among the
fruit barrows and corn bins, in the middle of the street,
it had seemed the most important thing she could do,
to use some of the money left from Godmother Fry's
gift, spend it extravagantly, like the woman who had
poured out the jar of precious ointments. She had to
give something to Ben, and not a useful gift, just an
object to touch and keep and wonder at. Though, on
the way home, she had been worried, for fear that he

might scorn her and care nothing at all for the stone. Perhaps she had bought it only for herself, her own pleasure. She kept putting her hand down to where it lay at the bottom of the basket, wrapped in newspaper, feeling the hard peaks, like a cluster of tiny needle mountains.

The weather had changed, it was like early spring, and even warm, as she walked the two miles up from the road in the late afternoon. There were aconites and celandines just pushing up through their green sheaths on the banks. Too early, Ben would say, the snow might come again yet, even in March or April. The woods and coppices were still leafless, branches openmeshed, or else pointing up, thin and dark against the blue-white sky; she could see all the way down between the wide-spaced beech trunks, to the fields below.

But there was something in the air, something, a new smell, the beginning of growth, and, as she walked, she had felt a great happiness spurt up within her, and the countryside had looked beautiful, every detail, every leaf-vein and grass-blade was clear and sharp, it was as though she had been re-born into some new world. There was a change in the light, so that the dips and hollows of the valley that she could see between the gaps in the hedges, as the track climbed higher, up to the common, had changed their shapes, and the colours changed, too, the bracken was soft moss-green and the soil gold-tinged like tobacco. Yesterday, it had been dark as peat.

She wanted to sing. Because she had all she could ever want, the whole earth belonged to her, and in the end, seeing the cottage ahead, she had had to shake her head to clear it, she was giddy with this happiness. She had to remind herself that nothing had really happened, had it, it was still winter – there was only the last of the warmth and light of the sun, over Laker's Wood.

She unpacked her basket slowly, but it stayed with her, this light-headedness, her eyes saw everything in the house itself as if for the first time. And then there was the rose-quartz lying on the wooden table.

Ben had not been scornful. He had examined the crystal, without touching it, for a long time, and then gone to the desk to find the magnifying glass his grandfather had given him years before, and together, standing near to the window, they had looked at each of the glittering points and smooth slopes.

'Jo would know about it. Where it came from, how it got fashioned.' Yes, that was the sort of thing Jo always knew.

She said, 'It didn't cost much and I took it out of my own money. I just wanted it for you.'

He seemed not to hear her. He never found it easy, to reply to affection, or to speak about what he himself felt.

'Where shall you put it?'

He hesitated. Shook his head, 'I'll think.'

So, for the time being, it had stayed there on the

table, she had looked at it again and again, as she cooked their meal.

That night, he had not tried to find a job to do in the house or the garden. He had eaten, and then read the paper she had brought back from the town, and after that, a book Tomkin the pharmacist had lent him, about change-ringing.

They had asked him to join the ringers a couple of years ago, just before he and Ruth were married, to fill the place left by old Riddock, and at first, Ben had been doubtful, it was something new, a skill quite unlike those natural to him. But they had seemed sure. He was even-tempered and he worked with his hands, Tomkin said, as well as being young and strong, and he'd grown up to the sound of the bells, he would have a feel for them. And so he had. The older men had all learned the changes by heart, and by working as a team for years together and so becoming sensitive to one another's movements and to all the rhythms and patterns. But Tomkin studied it by book, too, and thought Ben ought to do the same.

He read for an hour, and Ruth had watched him, and only been glad to enjoy this unusual quietness, which somehow linked itself with the happiness she had known, walking up the hill.

It had dropped down cold in the room. Ben had built up the fire with the last of the chestnut logs.

'It's not spring yet – there. Don't you forget it.'

But she had not believed him.

Nor could she the next morning, as he stood drinking his mug of tea and the dawn came seeping, white-grey as a ghost, up through the meadow and the garden.

'Frost,' Ben said, and pointed to where the sprout-tops gleamed faintly. The tea steamed up into his face.

By the time he left the sky was pink as raspberries, the sun coming up.

'Spring,' she said, 'you'll see.'

He shook his head, laughing, and when he opened the back door, the air came in cold and sharp as glass. She watched him walk away unhurried, the lunch-bag over his left shoulder, and again the happiness began to suffuse her like wine, she felt that she might do anything, anything in the world.

She cut the last of the stale loaf, and some bacon fat, and then filled the corn bucket, and went down to feed first the tits and blackbirds, and then the hens. It was the last day of February. Tomorrow meant March. 'Spring,' she said.

Balaam brayed softly from behind the fence and the hawthorn hedge and the branches of the apple trees were crowded with birds, singing, singing.

*

By mid-morning, it was warm again, the frost on the short grass had melted to pin-heads of water, glistening in the sun.

She worked in the kitchen with the door open, washing, making the bread, and then paused, to watch the long-tailed tits, swinging and swooping upside down like acrobats on their string. An ordinary day. Quiet, as it was always quiet here.

Carter came earlier than usual for the swill, and told her about the birth of another daughter to the curate's wife. She liked Carter, because he passed on news and never gossip, he never made scandal. A birth or death, disease among cattle, weather on the other side of the ridge. But nothing private, no half-truths or speculations. People trusted Carter.

The sun rose higher in a clear sky.

Just before four o'clock, she took the clothes basket and pegs and went down to the washing-line, slung between two of the apple trees. And it happened then. As she lifted up a shirt and shook it open, she felt as if she had been struck in the face; but it was not pain, it was a wave of terror, rising, breaking and pouring down over her, the sky seemed to have gone black. She felt faint at the impact of it, her hands shook so that she dropped the wet shirt on to the grass, and stood, her heart drumming. It was the first time in her life that she had known anything like it, such dread and foreboding, and she waited, wondering if she were ill. She had neither seen nor heard anything to make her afraid. But something had happened, some terrible thing, and now, she could hardly breathe, there was a squeezing in her chest and she panted for air, like the Riddock boy in one of his fits of asthma. What was it? She had her arm up, she was clutching on to the trunk of the tree, and dare not move, for if she moved, she felt that she herself, or else the whole world about her, might disintegrate. Her skin was cold, she was shivering and the blood seemed to be moving more and more slowly through her body, and to be held in suspension, dead as a pool of stagnant water, within the bowl of her skull. What was it that had come into the garden?

She had no idea of how long she stood there, nor how, at last, she managed to loosen her grasp upon the tree and walk back very slowly to the house, leaving the basket, and the white shirt where it had fallen, on the grass. She tried to pour herself some water but her hand trembled so much that she dropped the cup and broke it and looked down with renewed terror at the splintered pieces on the red tiled floor. She wanted to run away, get out of herself, out of this fear, and she could not move; she wanted to hide, in a cupboard or behind a chair, as she had hidden from thunderstorms, as a small child, to escape from what might be coming. The sight of the garden filled her with horror now, though it was the same, still in full sunlight, full of plants and trees and birds, and the donkey was there and the pecking, scratching hens. Oh, what had happened?

The tightness went from her chest, she began to

breathe more easily, but she only managed to get as far as a chair in the other room, and to sit on the very edge of it, all her nerves and muscles bunched up hard together. She put one hand on her wrist and felt her own pulse leaping irregularly, like the ticking of some crazy clock. The air smelled thick with her own fear.

The light was fading, the sky beyond the window had lost its translucence.

She would have to do something, pull herself together somehow and get up, go into the kitchen, begin preparing their meal. But at the idea of moving at all, it rose up again like sickness, the panic at what was happening to her mind and body and the recollection of the way it had come upon her, with such violence. If it was an illness, then how could she explain it, what pain or injury could she single out? There had been no pain, no, everything she felt had been shock and fear. And this certainty that something was wrong.

It was Colt who came, David Colt, the youngest of the foresters who worked for Rydal. He had been running uphill all the way from Helm Bottom, and when he reached the gate, he leaned on it to get his breath and to prepare himself. Young Colt, small and fair and thin, with bones that looked too fine and brittle for the work he did. Ruth saw him. Saw his face. Knew.

He came around to the back door, and started when she was there already, facing him, waiting. He put up a hand to wipe the sweat from his upper lip.

She said, 'Where is he?'

'He…'

'Where is he? What's happened to him? He's hurt, something… I knew he was hurt…'

He began to stammer, his hand still up to his face, he was breathless again.

'I wasn't there … I was … It was in Helm Bottom but I was farther up, on the slope … Potter … there was only Potter with him. I wasn't there.'

His tongue felt thick and swollen, like a cow's tongue, filling up his mouth.

'*Where is he?*'

'They're … they've had to get him down to the road – the doctor came…, they…'

He turned away from her abruptly, he thought, I don't know what to do, I can't say it, Jesus God, please why didn't they send someone else, why doesn't one of the others get here?

It was almost dark now. Colder.

Ruth cried out at him in anger, she wanted to shake him, to make him tell her.

'A tree fell…'

'He's gone to the hospital? They've taken him away? Where have they taken him? What are they doing to him?'

She must go, she had to be with him, that was all she could think of, she did not want anyone else to touch him in any way.

'It killed him. He's dead.'

Everything within her fell into place and she was still. She accepted it at once, and understood, remembering that she had known, known the moment it happened.

'The tree fell…. they …'

Then, the others came, Potter and another man, she saw the relief on David Colt's face, which was pale as marble. They seemed like giants moving towards her, giants with enormous arms and striding legs and bodies like rocks. Potter hesitated, and then moved Colt aside, touched Ruth's arm, to come into the house. She leaped back from him as though she had been scalded. He opened his mouth and began to speak, while the others stood silent behind him in the doorway, and that was when she had blocked her ears and begun to scream, she would not listen. She knew all she needed to know. Ben was dead. She wanted them to say nothing of how it had come about or what the falling tree had done to his body, she tried to drown it all, and the very sight of them, with her own screaming.

Potter stopped speaking. Led her into the other room, to a chair, lit the lamp. And then waited beside her until she, too, went quiet. One of the others had brought her a glass of water. She pushed it away.

'You get on back,' Potter said, 'I'll fetch her down. She'd best be at Bryce's now. The doctor can go there. I'll fetch her down.'

'NO!'

The others were going from the room.

'I'm staying here.'

'It's for the best. You'll need to be looked after.'

'No, no, no…'

He sighed.

'I'm all right. Ben's dead, I know. I knew when it happened. I knew. *I'm all right.*'

'You can't stop up here on your own.'

'Someone went to tell them? To Foss Lane?'

'Yes.'

'Leave me by myself.'

'I can't do that, how can I?'

Ruth looked up at Potter for a moment. She knew almost nothing about him, though Ben had worked with him for five years or more. He lived alone, across the common, always had.

'I don't want to go there. Be with them. I don't want that.'

She was aware of his distress, that he was shocked himself by what had happened, and at a loss to know how to cope with her, what to say or do that was right; he could not force her to move and feared to leave her alone.

She got up and went into the kitchen and made tea for them, she felt quite calm. So long as they did not try to tell her any more. Now that she knew he was dead, she no longer wanted to be with him, because wherever his body was, it was not Ben any longer. Ben was … She looked up. He was here. Somewhere here. She might put out a hand and touch him. If she spoke to him, he would hear her. The whole house was full of him. Ben.

They drank their tea and the fire spurted up, throwing a brick-red light on to Potter's face, and his thick hands, wrapped around the mug. Perhaps he would stay with her for a time. She wanted him to stay, now.

She said, 'It was like spring. I said that, this morning, I said ... he laughed at me. There was a frost when he went out but it came up warm, didn't it? Warm as spring.'

He did not reply. She could not explain to him about her happiness of the previous day and how the whole world had seemed new, nor about her terror in the garden.

She said, 'I knew.' But it meant nothing to him.

'Won't you go there? Let me fetch you down to the village. It'd be for the best.'

'No.'

He frowned and wished, as young Colt had wished, for someone else to come, to relieve him of the responsibility for her. He was never easy with other people, except children now and then. He had only seen Ruth at odd times, walking somewhere about, and nodded to her.

Inside his head, he heard over and over again, the creak and crash of the falling elm, and then the silence that had come over the whole wood. He saw himself bending down to the young man's body and knowing at once, knowing without having to touch. And it had been nobody's fault. Not his, not Ben's. An accident. Pointless. Done with.

It made him anxious to watch her, leaning a little towards the fire, not crying. But, because there was nothing else that he could do, he stayed with her, in the silence.

*

She lost count of how many people came up to the cottage that night, there seemed to be no end to them, all the long evening, no end to the sound of footsteps and the respectful knocks upon the door, the set faces – older and younger men, Mrs. Rydal and Carter's wife, and Alice Bryce. But they all seemed to be a great distance away from her, even as they filled up the small room, she heard what they said as though it came from down a long tunnel.

'Come back with us. You shouldn't stop here. It's the shock. You don't know what you're doing. It's not right to be on your own after this. It isn't what Ben would have wanted for you.'

She was appalled that they should think to know better than she did what he would want, and would have told them not to mention him at all, except that she knew, within her, that it did not matter, for she had Ben, all to herself, now, they could never reach him.

'I'm staying here. I'm all right. *Please.*'

She had not moved from the chair by the fire. Potter had long since gone.

'I'm all right.'

It exhausted her, it was like trying to make the deaf or the mad understand what she was saying.

Alice Bryce sat at the table, her face turned away from Ruth. Alice, almost as tall as Ben, and like him, in feature, though not in colouring or manner, nor at all in the person she was.

Proud, they had always said that of Ruth. But it was Alice who was proud, of her own beauty and grace of movement, and proud because of the way Dora Bryce had brought her up, the things she had made her believe about herself.

'You'll be what I never had the chance to be. I won't live to see you waste your life, throw yourself away on a man with no prospects, and stuck in a place like this, never having enough, never doing what you could have done. You're going to be somebody.'

She was wearing a dark blue dress, high up to her neck, and it suited her, showed off her hair and the sheen of her fair skin. Whatever money there was over, at Foss Lane, went on clothes for Alice.

'Go back,' Ruth said again. 'Go back home.'

For she needed more than anything to be alone with this vivid, certain awareness of Ben, all these people who came here were shutting him out, keeping him away from her.

'They had to get mother to bed. The doctor had

to come, give her something to make her sleep. She couldn't have come up here with me.'

'No.'

'Don't you care about us? What we feel? He didn't only belong to you. Don't you know what it was like for her, having them come to tell her like that?'

Ruth got up and went into the kitchen, and saw that the moon had risen and the light of it was shining on to the rose-quartz, which was still where Ben had left it, on the kitchen table. And something seemed to come from it and its beauty, so that, looking at it, she could take hold of herself again, and so forgive Alice for what she had said. She wanted to stay in the quiet, cold kitchen alone. While she was there, she did not feel so detached from everything; she held the knowledge that Ben was dead and yet here, with her, steadily in the front of her mind. She was not shocked or sick or afraid. Everything in the world was in pace. The clock ticked. They thought that she had not taken it in, they had all waited for her to collapse and begin to scream again, to depend upon them.

'You're not normal.'

Alice had said that, Ben's sister, sitting in the other room, Alice, who had no possible idea of how, in this one day, Ruth had utterly changed. From the moment of buying the piece of quartz at Thefton and the revelation of a new world in the sunlight as she had walked home up the hill, from then on, everything formed a pattern, as regular and beautiful as that of the crystal. A pattern only she could see.

Alice. She must go back, must speak to Alice again. Not to explain to her, no. But try and be kind, at least, to this girl who had never liked or accepted her. For none of them had been given what had come to her, the understanding of the pattern, completed at four o'clock, with Ben's dying. Whatever happened afterwards, she would not lose that knowledge, it might be all that, in the end, could save her.

'I'll make a drink for you?'

Alice stared. 'You haven't understood, have you? You're going about like someone asleep. Ben's dead. He is *dead*.'

And she beat her hands suddenly, down on the table.

'Yes.'

'You don't know, you haven't believed it yet.'

'There's tea. Or cocoa. I bought some cocoa at the market.'

'Don't you ...'

But then, she got up quickly, looked round for her coat. It was late now, past midnight. Nobody else had come.

'You said you wanted to be left. All right, I'll leave you. You don't need anything from me. Any of us. You never have.'

Ruth stood in the doorway, feeling sorry for Alice, and yet far away from her again, a world distant.

She said, 'There's a moon. You'll be able to see down the hill. You'll be all right.'

A log toppled over in the grate and the sparks splattered up, and then fell again, like a firework.

'There was a message,' Alice's voice was hard 'Is he to be brought here, when they've done, or come to Foss Lane? You're the one to say.'

'It doesn't matter.'

'Which?'

'Your mother...'

'She wants him home.'

'Then let her.'

For she did not want a coffin here, she did not want the body, she had all she wanted, Ben with her, and the house full of him, as he had been alive in it.

'It would be easiest.'

The words would hardly come out of her mouth, she was suddenly stupid with tiredness.

'From there. It's nearer.'

At the front door, Alice turned.

'You're not even crying. You've not even feeling enough to cry.'

Ruth went back to her chair, and slept at once, and the fire slipped down and darkened and died within the grate, so that when Jo came to her, just after six the next morning, the room was cold and without any comfort, in the first, thin light.

They would never have sent him up here, he must have

made his own decision to come, and then, nothing would have stopped him. When she opened her eyes, he was there, a few feet away, looking at her anxiously.

'Jo ...'

She moved, and all the muscles down her neck and back were aching, her left arm had gone numb, where she had leaned upon it.

The room looked the same, everything in its familiar place, and that surprised her for a moment, she had somehow expected it to be altogether changed.

'Jo,' she said again, and with pleasure, for he was the only person she wanted to be with – when she saw him, relief flooded her, because he would not try to make her do anything against her wishes, and there would be no need for explanations.

'You didn't go to bed.'

'But I did sleep. I didn't think I'd want to ... I couldn't get upstairs, I was so tired.'

She remembered the exhaustion, so great that her thoughts were incoherent, she had not known what she was doing.

'You wouldn't have been comfortable.'

'It didn't matter.'

They were silent, for a moment, looking at each other. But not because they were either of them afraid or embarrassed. There was no need for much speaking.

Jo went into the kitchen, she heard him open the range and begin to riddle out the cold ashes; he went outside for coal, filled the kettle.

He called through, 'I'll do the hens, in a minute, when this is going.'

'No.'

For she wanted to do something herself, and she wanted to see the hens. She took the scoop and filled it with meal. Jo did not argue. He accepted, always, what people said, respected them.

The hens were restless inside the coop, waiting like a gaggle of school-children for the gates to be unlocked, they came out and flapped around her legs, bumping up against one another, as she mixed the meal and water. It seemed a hundred years since yesterday morning, when she had come down to do this same job, after Ben had left for work.

Then there were the eggs, several of them still warm. She put them into the empty scoop and, lying there in a clutch together, pale brown and creamy grey, they were like the beach stones Jo had collected, on a holiday the family had taken, when he was six. The Bryces had had some money then, put by over the years, and they had all of them gone forty miles on the train from Thefton, to the sea. Jo had told her about it, he remembered every detail, the five days' holiday still shone out in magic splendour from the past. That was before Ruth had come here, and it was a time she liked to hear about, because anything that had happened in Ben's life was important to her, she wanted to link herself with it in her imagination.

It had only been a month afterwards that Arthur

Bryce had been gored by the bull, and though he went back to work for Rydal eventually, it was only on odd jobs, the money wasn't the same and so there had been no more holidays.

'I could fry an egg for you,' Jo said, when she brought them in, 'The range is getting up all right.'

'No.'

He didn't press her.

'But you have one. You get some breakfast, Jo.'

'I came straight out when I woke. The others weren't up.'

'Alice was here until late.'

'Yes. And then they went on all night, crying and everything. I kept hearing them.'

He selected an egg.

'You didn't cry, Ruth.'

'No.'

Jo – how could he be only fourteen and know so much, be so sure of what to do, how to talk to her? He was small for his age, and he had his father's build, broad-shouldered and with wide-spread hands and feet. It was Ben and Alice who were tall and light-boned like their mother.

He cooked two eggs with great care, basting them with fat, until the membrane over the yolks went milky and opaque. Was there nothing he could not do? And do well, because he was patient and thorough. He went to the cupboard for a plate, paused, glanced at her. Ruth shook her head. But it pleased her to watch

Jo eating the eggs, with bread and butter, his face serious and yet calm – they were both of them at ease.

She had met Jo only a few days after the first time she saw Ben, and an affection and understanding had at once been born between them. Jo had told her about the hoopoe he had seen in the woods, near Charnley, and how he had gone numb with the excitement of it, the bird was so rare and beautiful, with its exotic plumage and crest.

'No one believed me,' he had said, 'I wished I'd not told them. They all went out, right through the woods looking for it. Well, I knew they wouldn't see it, they made too much of a noise, you don't get to see anything that way. They said I'd been day-dreaming, only they meant lying. But it was a hoopoe. I know it was, I saw it.'

The next day, he had brought a bird book to show her, to Godmother Fry's cottage, where she was staying.

'It belonged to my great-grandfather.' He turned over the pages with immense care. 'There's a lot of his things in our house. Nobody else bothers with them.'

The book was heavy, bound in wine-red leather and with thin sheets of tissue paper covering each picture. They were tinted engravings, with all the fine details of feather-patterns and colours. They looked for a long time at the drawing of the hoopoe.

'I mayn't see one again,' Jo said, 'never in my life. They hardly ever come. But I did see it, that once. It's not a thing you could forget.'

Jo knew where there were kingfishers, too, in the stream that ran through the farthest edge of Rydal's woods, he had taken her there, one hot, still afternoon and taught her how to move, without disturbing anything. The blue of their wings caught the sun, reflected off the surface of the bright water.

'I don't tell people where they are,' Jo said, 'I come here by myself.'

'But you brought me.'

'Oh yes.'

'Aren't you afraid I'd tell someone?'

Jo looked away across the stream, to the far bank, where it sloped upwards, 'Not you,' he said, 'You wouldn't.'

It had been the first secret between them, and Ruth had wanted to say something to thank him, but could not find the words. And that was three years ago, Jo had only been eleven, a small boy, his hair cut short as hay-stubble, and yet there had been even then this wisdom in him, and a confidence about the world.

He finished the eggs, washed and dried the plate. Ruth stood beside the table. The memory of the walk home from the market, and of the last evening spent with Ben, lay like a beam of sunlight over the darker things in her mind. She felt oddly suspended, separate from the world. Time had stopped, at the moment in the garden when she had known about Ben's dying. She could not imagine how it would begin again.

Joe was touching the piece of crystal with the tips of his broad fingers.

'Rose-quartz.'

'Yes. I got it in Thefton. It was a present for Ben.'

'There's yellow quartz, like butter, you can find that, too, and white and blue. But blue's rare.'

Ben had said that Joe would know all about it.

'It might get knocked off there. It would be damaged. You could put it up on the desk.'

'No. I want it there.'

Nothing must change, nothing. She realised that Ben might have died a day sooner and never seen the crystal, never known that she wanted him to have a gift. But it was all right.

As soon as the range was hot, she went for a bath, pulling off her clothes in a frenzy, because she had been wearing them all the previous day and night, she felt unclean in them.

When the hot water came up and over her body, she felt that she might melt, or else be carried a long distance away, on this gentle, buoyant tide, and that was what she would have liked; it soothed her to soap her arms and legs and stomach and rinse the skin. It was like being bathed by someone else, as a child.

She thought, 'As long as I lie here, as long as this water is all around me, nothing bad can come about.'

She closed her eyes and saw colours behind the lids, limpid greens and blues, and then a light, pale and silvery as a star in the far distance. Her legs were weight-less, floating on the water. Perhaps this was drowning, and if it was, she would welcome it, there would be no fear or pain, no struggle. She was aware of Ben, very near to her, and he was frowning slightly, not angry, but puzzled. She tried to stretch a hand out to touch his face but he moved away, just out of reach. It did not alarm her, she was content to lie here in the water forever, to wait for him.

'Ruth…'

The voice came from somewhere else.

'Ruth.'

And then a tapping on the door. She opened her eyes, and could not think who it might be. Nobody must come here.

'Can't you hear me? Are you all right? Ruth?'

Jo.

The water had gone quite cold, with a cloudy scum filming the surface. The skin of her fingers was white and crinkled.

'I'm all right.'

'I'm just going to take some water to the donkey.'

She had forgotten the donkey's existence.

She got out of the bath, fully awake now, and cold. The white walls and porcelain of the sink and bath, the glass of the window, were too bright, burning her eyes, she wanted to put up a hand to shield herself from the glare of them, and the towel felt coarse and grainy, chafing her skin as she dried it. She had emerged from a dream in which there had been warmth and safety, into this bleak room. It was too real to be borne.

*

'We could play a game,' Jo said. 'Draughts, or dominoes, if you like.'

Outside, it was raining a little, a fine, misty rain, the sky was seagull grey. It was afternoon, she thought, or a bit later, she could not tell. Jo had eaten some cold meat and she had drunk milk, and then tea again; the hours seemed to be filled up with the sound of the hissing, boiling kettle, the taste and smell of the dark, soaked leaves. When she was not drinking tea, her mouth was dry as chalk.

What had Jo said? She looked at his face, trying to remember. No. The rain slid like silk down the window-pane.

'Jo, I don't want them to come here again. Not anyone. I don't want to see them.'

'No.'

'If they come here...' She clenched her fist tightly until the nails hurt her palms.

'It's all right. I'll tell them.'

'But will you stay, Jo?'

'Oh yes.'

'Yesterday ... last night ...' She took a deep breath, forming the words with care, inside her head, before speaking them aloud.

'Were you there? When they came to Foss Lane, after it happened? Did they tell you?'

'I opened the door. It was Mr. Rankin.'

She tried to picture it.

'My mother fainted, they had to give her brandy and the smelling salts. They had to put her to bed.'

He spoke of her with detachment, as though of a stranger.

'And you? What did you do?'

She was afraid that no one had thought to look after him, give him comfort.

'I went out. I walked, right up on to the ridge and over the other side. I walked a long way.'

'By yourself?'

'Yes. I was thinking. That was all. I didn't want to cry. I wanted to be by myself and think.'

He remembered it. In his pocket, there had been the bone handled pen-knife Ben had given him last birthday, and he had pressed it with his fingers, every so often, for reassurance.

The countryside, over the ridge, had been quite empty and peaceful, in the last of the sun. He had lain down on the grass on his stomach and looked over the small fields, rising one upon the other like green pillows, and at the bitter, brown clumps of woodland between. In the far distance, mauve and blue-grey, and receding as the light faded, the downs and barrows of the next county.

Jo said, 'It seemed ...' But stopped, for how could

he explain to her, that odd sense of rightness he had had, as though something had fitted together – it had been missing, like the piece of a puzzle, and was now in its proper place. He had never thought of death like that. It made no sense, how could it? He ought to feel anger and loss, and that everything had disintegrated, there was no point or purpose anywhere discernible. How could he tell her?

'I knew when it happened,' Ruth said. 'I was in the garden, and I thought ... it was as though I was dying, myself. I was afraid. I knew something terrible was happening.'

'People do know, sometimes. Animals know, as well.'

'How, Jo? How did I know?'

But she did not really need his answer. Loving Ben had meant being able to read his thoughts, to tell, wherever he was, however far away, what he was feeling, if he were happy or not. And so it had been with his dying.

Jo got up and drew the curtains.

'Don't they want you back? Shouldn't you go home?'

'Do you want me to?'

'No.'

'Well ... they don't bother.'

'You told them where you were?'

'I left a note. But it's nothing much to them, what I do.' It did not seem to trouble him.

He found the board and they played draughts, sitting close up to the fire, hearing the rain. Ruth felt as though she was outside of herself, another person, looking on at this girl in the wheat-coloured blouse and skirt; it was not her own hands which pushed the little red discs from square to square. Jo played the game well, and honestly, not holding back in order to let her win, and so she did not win, not once, which did not matter. Nothing mattered.

'Are you tired?'

The two people she had been, merged together again, at the sound of his voice.

'I don't know.'

'Should I get you something to eat now?'

'No.'

But when he had made his own meal, she picked a lump of cheese off the plate, and half a tomato, and they were enough, they satisfied her, though they tasted of nothing in her mouth.

'I'll sleep here, if you want me to,' Jo said.

Sleep. Yes, she could sleep again. But not upstairs – she could not face that room, with the bed, and all the drawers and cupboards full of Ben's clothes, and the smell of his hair left on the pillow. She would stay down here, sleep in the upright fireside chair again. And if she did not sleep, at least she would have the comfort of Jo's presence in the house.

'I'll make a bed for you. In the small room.'

'I can do it.'

'No.'

For she must not simply sit and sit, as though the blood was dammed up within her.

As she opened the door of the small room, it was again as though she had come face to face with Ben. She said his name aloud. A slight breeze puffed the cotton curtain, bringing in the smell of rain-soaked bracken and turf.

'Ben?'

The sky seemed full of him too, and he was part of the breaths she drew in, but he was also standing just behind her, looking over her shoulder. She wondered why she was not afraid, not of him, but of these things which she had never believed could happen. It was not the same as remembering Ben, or picturing him in her mind, it was a knowledge, that he was there. And most of all, he was there at moments when she had not been thinking of him: as she had come into this room, she had only been wondering which sheets to put on the bed for Jo, and whether it was at all damp.

She said, 'Ben. I'm all right. Nothing else can happen. I can't be hurt. You're here, and Jo is here. It is all right.'

Why did she speak to him? Ben was dead and gone away, was with God. But not here, in this room. Not here.

Yet he was here. She closed the curtain and wiped the beads of rain off the ledge. And thought, only let it stay like this, only let the clock stand still and let me feel no more than I feel now, let me have this reassurance. If it stays like this, I can bear it.

But she knew that it would not stay, that this was only a calm, to accept and be grateful for, something to hold to, before the coming of the storm.

*

That night, she scarcely slept at all. The exhaustion and shock had drained out of her like anaesthetic, she felt as though some great tide had thrown her up on to a beach and left her, wide awake. It was still raining. Ben had been right then, the spring had not come yet, and the two days of clear skies and sunlight seemed years away, a memory from childhood.

She had no sense, now, of Ben's presence in the house. She tried to recapture it, spoke to him again, but the room was empty. And now, she could not stop thinking about where they had taken him, after the accident, and what they were doing to his body.

She imagined how it might have been, wondered what they did to prepare a man for his coffin. She had never been in contact with the events of a death. Godmother Fry had died in her sleep, the week after Ruth had returned home, and the death of her mother had been years ago, when she was only three, they had shielded her from it completely, sent her away, to cousins in Derbyshire.

She supposed he was in the mortuary at the hospital, lying – lying where? On a bed or a stretcher? Or on a slab of marble? How did he look? Was he like Ben, or was he utterly changed, stiff and pale, like the dead piglet they had once found by a gateway? Ben had picked it up, and buried it in their own garden, under the apple trees. She had watched him. Now they would bury Ben. Perhaps he was bandaged, or already sewn into the cotton shroud. Other people had touched him, people who had no rights, they had been strange, impersonal hands which had undressed him and washed his body, closed his eyelids, and she resented them, he was hers, no one else should have violated him in that way. Because her feeling that his body was nothing, an empty shell, had left her, she could not think of him now, except in terms of flesh and blood and hair and bone, a living body. What she most desperately wanted to know she dare not ask; if the tree had broken open his head, or fallen on his chest, crushing the rib cage, and the lungs and heart pulsing inside it. And what did they do? Did they mend the fractures and stitch up the open wounds of a dead body, or leave it as it was, because there would be no point?

On Thursday, he would be brought to Foss Lane. It was what Dora Bryce wanted, and Ruth had said, and meant it, that it did not matter to her. But now, it did matter, now she wanted him here, wanted to touch him, to sit beside him as long as she could. He belonged here.

Ratheman, the curate, had come over about the funeral, and to speak to her, but she had fled upstairs and hidden in the small room, he had been forced to leave a message with Jo. Why had she been so afraid to see him? He was a good man, and she believed what he believed. But she did not want him to talk to her, about Ben's dying, and being reborn into eternal life, for she knew it already, and what she did not know, she would discover in her own way, by herself.

The funeral was on Friday, and someone would fetch her, 'No. I can walk there. I'd rather that.'

Jo looked anxious.

"What is it?"

'You ought to ... they want you to go to the house first. Then everybody's together, walking behind, up to the church.'

Everybody together. She did not want to be with any of them. She resented the people's grief, and knew how keen it would be, for everyone had loved Ben, everyone would feel the loss. But she wanted to be the only one who mourned him, the only one who was bereft.

The funeral loomed ahead of her like some terrible cliff face which she must climb, for there was no way round or back. She sat, gripping the arms of the chair, and prayed for strength to bear it all, without losing her reason.

At first, she did not understand the cry that came from

upstairs. She had been locked up within herself unaware of the room and the darkness, the last heat from the core of the fire.

Then she jumped up. Jo was here. It was Jo.

He was sitting up in bed holding his hands over his face.

'Jo...'

He did not move. The room smelled damp.

Ruth sat on the bed and touched his arm, but when, at last, he took his hands away, she saw that he had not been crying, as she had supposed, his eyes were dry, and huge in his wide-boned face, the skin was taut and gleaming with fear.

'Jo ... it's all right, I'm here. What happened?'

For a time, he did not reply, or appear to feel her touch.

Then, he breathed very deeply several times, and lay back.

'I was dreaming, I didn't know where I was.'

'You're here.'

'It was the trees.'

She waited, afraid of what she would hear. 'I was in the wood somewhere. It was beautiful – sunny and quiet, you know how it is? I was happy and all the trees had faces and the faces were laughing. I was laughing.'

He took another breath and shivered slightly. Ruth touched her fingers to the side of his face.

'Then it went dark and all the faces changed. They were ugly faces, leering, like those gargoyles on the church tower, they were devils. They were all coming down on me, and I'd fallen, I couldn't get away.'

Nightmares. But perhaps, in the end, they might help him to work out his grief and fear. All hers were to come.

'Should I make a drink?'

'What time is it?'

She did not know.

'But I'll sit here with you. I'll make us some cocoa.' By the time she returned, Jo's face had relaxed, there was some colour in it and his eyes were no longer wide with the recollection of his terror.

He said, 'What will you do, Ruth? Afterwards? What will happen to you?'

Afterwards? She had not thought of it, such a time did not yet exist.

'I shouldn't want you to go away.'

'Away? No ... Oh, no.'

For even if she could bear the idea of it, where was there to go? This was her home, she belonged nowhere else now.

She had come three years ago to stay with Godmother Fry, after the wedding of her father and Ellen Gage. Ellen, who was kind to her, wanted to love her and be accepted, who would make a good wife for him. Ruth had been happy about it, most of all because now she could be free, she was not the only person her father lived for, he no longer wanted to tie her to him. She liked Ellen, but, after the marriage, she had wanted to come away, to prove to herself that it was possible, now that she was eighteen, a person in her own right.

Godmother Fry had been almost ninety by then, and half-blind, she walked with a stick. But there had never been anyone so full of vigour and courage, and she cared about others, interested herself in them, so that the house was always full of visitors, being happy in her company. She had welcomed Ruth as a child of her own, and Ruth, in return, had cooked and done work about the house, and taken the old woman out, to walk slowly through the village. It was June, high summer, the backs of the men haymaking in Rydal's top fields were burnt brown as toffee. It seemed like home then, even before she met Ben.

'Where could I go, where else is there, Jo?'

He set his empty mug down on the shelf.

'Did I tell you about the shells?'

She blinked. But this was typical of him, he always expected people to have followed his quick changes of thought.

'I found them in the attic cupboard. They were shells my great-grandfather brought back from the West Indies and China. Some of them look as if they were made of pearl, and there's a pink one, coiled like a snake. I'm going to read about them.'

Shells. Shells and stones, birds and plants and insects and the fungi that grew in the damp, secret crevices of the woods – Jo knew about them all.

'I'd like to go to those places.' His voice was becoming drowsy. 'I'd like to be a sailor. Think of what I'd see.'

'Shouldn't you miss it here? Everything you've always known?'

'Yes. And so I don't know what I'll do. There are countries I read about, hot places, where the birds are all bright as parrots, flying about among the trees, just like sparrows and things here. And jungle rivers and forests. And storms, going round Cape Horn. All of that ... sometimes, it's all I want.'

He opened his eyes. He was rested. But he said, 'What about you, Ruth? What about you?'

She shook her head, and after a moment, left him. And stood on the landing opposite the door of the room she dared not enter.

It was almost four o'clock. She slept a little, restlessly, and took on Jo's dream, so that she flinched back from the faces of the trees and the way they threatened her, and then, she saw that they wore the expressions of all those people who had been up here since yesterday, Potter and Alice, David Colt, the curate, and others, too, the ones she had still to see, Dora and Arthur Bryce, and all the people of the village. It seemed to last for hours, but when she woke again, it was only just after five. She sat, letting the nightmare wash over her and recede gradually, until her head was rinsed clean and clear of all things, memories, faces, fears.

She watched the hands of the clock move from five to half past, to six, and then seven, when Jo came quietly into the room.

Now it was Thursday. Only another day and another night, only this small amount of precious time, like a globule of water hanging from a tap, but ready to fall, to burst open.

In the kitchen, Jo filled the range and put the kettle on to boil. The sounds comforted her.

*

It was just after five o'clock. She rinsed her hands and face at the tap in the kitchen, and the water was icy, burning her skin.

In that time between the fading of moonlight and the rising of dawn, everything about her seemed curiously insubstantial, and she herself felt weightless, as though she were in a dream. But the long grass at the side of the path brushed against her legs like damp feathers. The world was real enough.

The path led out into the lane, which sloped for a mile, between the beeches. All the night animals had retreated into nests and burrows, and as she came up to the field gate, the first birds were making individual, exploratory calls.

The sky paled a little and now she saw the mist, like soft grey bundles of wool left about at the bottom of the meadow, and on the margin of the wood. The grass smelled sappy and fresh as she trod it down, and the mist gave off its own peculiar, raw smell as she passed through it.

Inside the wood, the ground sloped sharply downhill, and was a mulch of wet leaves and moss and soil, she had to hold on to branches and roots, to steady herself. But every moment, it was growing lighter, now she could see the grey outline of trees, a few yards ahead. She felt nothing, was not afraid, she only concentrated upon getting there.

Lower down there was more mist, trailing about her like tattered chiffon scarves. The beeches gave way to oak and elm, with low bushes and briars. A weasel streaked across the path ahead of her, red eyes gleaming like berries. Then, another slope down to the last clearing. It was very still here. Everything was gradually taking on its own colour again, as the first light filtered through, the various shades of grey separated themselves from one another, and the brown of soil and dead leaf, the silvery fringed lichen and mould-green moss.

Helm Bottom.

At first, she saw nothing to indicate that this was the place. And then, behind her, the pile of cut-down undergrowth and pruned branches, laid together.

The tree itself was a few feet away, the roots had been half torn-out of the ground like teeth from a gum, leaving a ragged hole. When she went close to it, she could see that the wood was rotten, a honeycomb of dead, dry cells running through its core. But the outer branches looked healthy, there were buds forming. It had been nobody's fault, no one could have known.

Very slowly, she crouched down and put her hands on the tree bark. It was faintly spongy with moss. So this was it. This. Though she had no way of telling which part of it had fallen on to him, the ground was trampled and churned up, where all the men had been, he might have lain anywhere.

She understood that it had been utterly right for Ben to die here, in the wood. Because it was his place, he had known it since childhood, he was a forester. She was grateful. She would not have wanted him sick, in bed for months in some strange hospital. Everything was well.

A thin dart of sunlight came between two branches and caught on a cobweb laid out on the hawthorn, the tiny water-beads were iridescent. She was stiff and cold, kneeling there, she could feel the damp soaking through her clothing, but she did not go, she laid her face against the fallen tree, and it gave her some sort of courage, some sort of hope. She half-slept, and pictures shuffled like cards before her eyes, she heard the bird-song and then it was confused with snatches of human speech, so that she thought they had all come for her, were surrounding her, in the wood.

When she opened her eyes again, she knew something more. That this was a good place, because Ben had died here and he had been good. 'Whenever she came here, it could only give her peace, she could not be assailed by any fear, nothing could harm her here. For if a bad death haunted a place with evil, why should not a good death imprint its own goodness?

It was a long time before she got up, and tried to bring back some warmth to her cramped limbs.

The mist had folded back and back upon itself like a long pillow at the bottom of Low Field. She found mushrooms, more than a dozen of them, with their delicate pink-brown grilles and tops of white suede, she put some in her pockets and carried the rest between cupped hands back up the hill and across the common, to where she found Jo waiting, full of alarm, by the gate. She called out, to reassure him, and the donkey heard her, too, and brayed.

'Ruth…'

'It's all right.'

'Mushrooms!'

'I found them in Low Field.'

He glanced at her quickly.

'I went there. To Helm Bottom. I had to go.'

'Yes.'

'I had to go by myself.'

'Is it all right?'

'Yes.'

Yes, for now, she had something to hold on to, some

kind of reassurance which would take her through this
day. It was only the end of it she dreaded, and dared
not look beyond, for the worst would come to her, she
knew, when, for everyone else, it was all over.

3

As she turned into Foss Lane and saw the house, she had again the sensation of being outside her own body, of watching her own actions with interest but without emotion. There were people round the doorway, but they moved back, murmuring a little and then falling silent, as they saw her. She was wearing the brown skirt and coat, and no hat, because she did not possess a hat, and it had not occurred to her to buy one specially. That would have changed her, she would not be the person Ben knew.

At the open door, she paused, and her heart began to beat violently, she gripped her hands together.

There they were. All of them, in black, and the women in hats, the men formal and unfamiliar in suits, with arm-bands. And as she entered the tiny front room, they, too, fell silent. Nobody came to her.

Dora Bryce was in a chair beside the fire, a hand-kerchief to her face. The room was hot. Ruth felt that she would choke, she wanted to run away from these ashen, sepulchral faces, What had any of this to do with her, or with Ben? She remembered what Jo had told her, about people in the early church who wore white at a funeral for rejoicing.

'Ruth ...'

Arthur Bryce took her arm, and then let it go, awkwardly. His neck looked red and swollen under the stiff white collar.

Perhaps he did not dislike her, perhaps, if it had not been for the women, he might have been her friend, But he went along with them, Dora and Alice, did what they did.

Who were all the others? They looked curiously alike; they must be aunts and uncles and cousins of the Bryces. None of them was related to her. They either glanced at her and away quickly, or else stared with set faces. She thought, you've heard about me, and what you have heard you believe, there isn't anything they will not have told you.

Where was Jo? If Jo would come ... She had never felt so lonely, so set apart from other people, in her life, and she had only her own courage and pride to rely on.

'You'll want to come up.'

Arthur Bryce was standing in the doorway, at the foot of the stairs and for a moment she did not understand. When she did, she stepped back, the room tilted and her ears rang.

'Oh, no,' she said. 'No.'

Dora Bryce lifted her head.

'You're not going to pay your respects? You don't even want to say goodbye to him?'

'There's nothing to be afraid of. I'll come with you, girl.'

Arthur Bryce fingered his collar. 'He looks ...'

'No!'

She saw the expression on Alice's face, remembered what she had said that night. 'You've not even feeling enough to cry.' But she could not go upstairs, the sight of his body, lying in a coffin, which would soon be sealed up forever, would be more than she could bear. And it would mean nothing, now. She looked around the room. So they had all been up? Yes. She imagined the file of dark mourners mounting the stairs and peering down into the coffin. At Ben. Ben. How could they? How could so many people have touched him and looked at him, unasked, since the moment of his death, when she herself had not?

But it was better. She thought, they don't have Ben. When I last saw him, he was alive, walking up the path, at the beginning of an ordinary day, and we were happy, and that is what I want to remember, there is no strange, dead image to lie like a mask over that.

Dora Bryce was speaking, but her head was bent, the words were muffled and distorted with tears.

'There's a bed made up for you. For tonight.'

'No, I'll go back home.'

'Up there? You want to be alone up there tonight?'

Oh God, Oh God, it was all going to begin again, she wanted to scream at them, leave me alone, leave me alone!

'It'd be only right for you to stay with us this once. Today of all days.'

Why?

'Isn't it the least you can do?' Alice said, her voice ringing out clear and impersonal across the room.

Why? Why should it matter to any of them that she should stay here, under this roof, tonight? Why should it be unkind or disrespectful of her to go back to her own home?

Nothing more was said, because there were footsteps, the men in black overcoats were coming through the doorway and passing by her, on their way upstairs. Ruth thought, I could go, I could still go up, this is the last chance. She saw that Arthur Bryce was looking at her, expecting it.

She turned away. Saw the one car outside in the lane, and the clutch of onlookers, waiting, to stare and to follow behind the family, through the village and up to the church.

Someone had closed the inner door, but she could still hear it, from upstairs, the dull thud-thud of the hammer.

*

The car moved off very slowly, with two of the undertaker's men walking in front, and behind it, the column of mourners like black ants, and as they turned out of Foss Lane, the sun came out from behind full-bellied rain clouds. Ruth felt calm, and withdrawn from it all. She walked alone, needing no one. Jo was a pace behind her, watching, anxious. The wood of the coffin was pale as honey. It seemed to have nothing to do with Ben, because Ben was here, was all around her, was walking next to her, and occasionally, he touched her arm for comfort. She wanted to say, 'You went away and now you have come back. Where did you go? Why? Why?' She wondered if she was going out of her mind.

They were waiting at the lych-gate of the flint-faced church, the rector and the curate, like magpies in black and white, and suddenly, she remembered the day she and Ben had been married, remembered walking up here, early in the morning, dressed in plain, cream wool, without a hat or gloves or flowers. It had been a brief wedding, with only half a dozen people there, and afterwards, they had gone straight to the cottage, there had been no party. That was what they both wanted, and they did not care what conclusions the village might draw from the sudden, private ceremony: and Dora Bryce had had no choice but to agree, though she blamed Ruth for it all, for turning Ben against her.

The bell was tolling, and unconsciously, they began to walk in time with it, and everything in the world seemed to be slowing down, her own breathing and the beats of her heart, as well as the steps of the priests and the bearers, and soon, they would stop, it would all stop.

For a moment, it did, time ceased, as the men who had set the coffin down stepped back, and everyone found a place, and the two priests waited for the tolling bell to cease. The church was full. The bell ceased. The church seethed with silence.

Ruth was alone, beside Jo, in a pew in front of everyone else, so that she could only hear the noises of sobbing, the coughs and the shuffling feet, she did not have to look at their faces. Jo sat like a stone.

The priest was speaking, Ruth heard the words very clearly, very distinctly, and yet could find no meaning in them, they were in some foreign tongue. All her senses had become more acute, everything seemed hard-edged and perfectly defined in shape, her ears picked out the sound of every separate person's breathing.

Then, it burst upon her, as overwhelmingly as on the way home from Thefton market. There seemed to be a light within everything, the stones of the church walls and the dark wood of the pulpit, the white and yellow flowers on the coffin, the stained glass windows, the brass rail, everything shone and was caught up together in some great beauty, and all things were part of a whole. The pattern had fallen into place again, and the meaning of all things was ringing in her head, she could tell them, she could tell them, and then, at last, she heard words which she understood.

'Then I saw a new heaven and a new earth, for the first heaven and the first earth had passed away, and the sea was no more. And I saw the holy city, new Jerusalem, coming down from God out of heaven, prepared as a bride adorned for her husband: and I heard a great voice from the throne saying, "Behold the dwelling of God is with men. He will dwell with them and they shall be his people and God himself will be with them. And he will wipe every tear from their eyes and death shall be no more, neither shall there be mourning nor crying nor pain any more, for the former things have passed away."

This it was that set her apart from them, as she stood at the front of the church with her dark red hair loose over her shoulders, this revelation that she shared with Ben. Who was here, here. She felt faint, not with grief but with joy, because love was stronger than death.

*

The wind blew into their faces and stirred the funeral flowers and the heads of the poplars behind the church, and the clouds were fast-moving, heavy with rain to come.

When the clods of soil fell lightly on to the pale coffin lid, she thought that if she were to kneel down now, and prise it open, the box would be empty. She could not imagine how they believed, as they did, all black as crows, around the grave, that Ben was dead. She saw that they were watching her and thinking that she had still not accepted the truth, or else that it was her pride which kept her from crying. But how could she cry? Why should there be any reason for it? Their faces were all lifeless, carded and blotched with weeping, she wanted to shout out to them, 'You are the dead people. You!' For they seemed not to belong to any life she knew about, there was no link between them and the vibrant, dancing colours of the flowers and grasses and the holy breath of the wind, and the blood coursing through her own body.

Someone was touching her. Jo. People were moving away. It was finished. She looked at the rust-dark soil, piled up neatly on either side of the open grave.

'Ruth ...'

Jo had been crying, his eyes were dark as bruises. She took his hand and felt the trembling in it, and they came a long way behind the others, away from the churchyard.

People hovered, perhaps waiting to speak to her, tell her what they themselves felt, but seeing her face, they dropped back or turned aside and remained silent.

Dora Bryce was walking unsteadily, clinging to her husband's arm, and to Alice on the other side, and so it was around her that people gathered, for they knew what to do with a woman who wept or fainted, who behaved in the way that seemed right, because customary.

Again, they were all crowded into the front room. Ruth watched them as they began to relax, in their

unfamiliar clothes, and were easier, talking to one
another, now that the coffin had gone from the house.
She saw their hands reach out for sandwiches and small
cakes, their fingers stirring spoons round and round,
in the best china cups. Jo sat beside her, not speaking, and after a while, they stopped pressing her to eat
or drink, they ignored her, out of embarrassment or
mistrust. The afternoon trailed on and none of them
went home and their voices rose and fell and buzzed
about like insects trapped in her ears. The tiredness
came back, deadening her limbs, she had not the will
or energy to try, again, to return home. Her eyelids felt
swollen and sore. She could not move, she might never
move again.

*

The room was empty. They were all of them gone.
The table was a mess of empty plates and doilies and
spoons. The silence brought her back to herself.

She let Alice take her up the stairs and into the
bedroom they had made ready for her. It was very
clean and cold, very small, there were no ornaments or
pictures, and the sheets were bound tight as bandages
over the bed.

Knowing that she would not sleep, she did not
bother to disturb them, nor to undress, except for
her shoes and stockings They were forcing her to
take part in some curious ritual of their own and

she had no strength left in her to battle with them. But what good she could be doing, what duty she fulfilled by spending this one, enforced night in the house of her dead husband's family, she could not fathom. Did not try. Her brain ached with tiredness and with the emotions that had overtaken her, one after another and so completely, in the course of the past four days.

Nobody came to her, and she did not want any false gestures of friendship. But, lying on the high, narrow bed, and hearing the movements all about the house, she wanted someone, anyone, some touch or word.

For the beginning of the night, she listened to the keening of Dora Bryce, it came to her as clearly as if there were no walls to the house. It was a terrible noise, she was ashamed of the woman for making it, and ashamed of herself, because she could not. It rose and fell, in a mad, distracting rhythm of its own, and then, in the aftermath, a muffled sobbing, and the rumble of Arthur Bryce's voice. There were footsteps up and down the staircase. Alice was there with her mother, and she too was crying. Ruth's body was rigid. The night was the length of all the nights she had ever lived through. Outside, the wind made a thin, high sound of its own, as it passed by the house.

Once, she got up and looked out of the window, and saw steely clouds moving fast over the face of the full moon, and the words of a ballad about death jazzed inside her head.

'They planted an apple tree over his head,
Hum. Ha. Over his head.'

Dora Bryce's crying died away, the house was quiet.
Then, Ruth might have cried. But would not, not
here. There was some pride damming up her own
grief, she would not let them hear, as they had not
been able to see, earlier, what she felt.

It seemed more than ever strange, that this family
should be Ben's, that someone like him should have
come from such people. Or Jo, for Jo did not belong
here either. Only Alice was at one with them, only she
had inherited their narrowness and lack of heart.

Ben had brought her to Foss Lane a week after they
met. Because already, after that short time, they knew,
both of them, their future was as inevitable as that the
trees should continue to grow. He had called for her,
on a Sunday afternoon, at Godmother Fry's, and Ruth
had been anxious in case what she was wearing was not
right, was too formal or else too plain, was showy – in
some way unsuitable. Ben had laughed at her. 'It's
you,' he said, 'they're going to meet you, aren't they?
They won't mind what you wear, they won't notice.'

But he must have known that that was not true,
that her dress and every detail about her, hair and
shoes and bracelet, would be what they saw first, and
scrutinised, and judged her by. She had wanted to be
friendly, become a part of them. Now, she knew that

no matter how she had looked, what she had worn or said or done, none of it would have made any difference, they had disliked her in advance. Any girl who might take Ben away could not be approved of, or accepted.

This afternoon had brought it back to her, because it had been the same. They had sat on the edges of uncomfortable chairs in the front room, drinking tea out of the best china cups, and Ruth had been unable to think of anything at all to say to them, and so had remained silent, and they had taken that for pride, she was branded for life with that one word. She remembered the way they had looked at her, and how Ben, too, had fallen silent, unable to help her, and only Jo had been himself, talking about a place he knew of, where you might find wild raspberries.

She thought, now I will never come to this house again. There is no love, no kindness, no friendship to bind me to them, and they will be glad of that. I will die to them, as Ben has died. No, more, because they will hoard their memories of him and cling to them, as people keep old letters, Dora Bryce will cling to the past, before I married Ben, she will indulge her own grief and self-pity for the rest of her life, but she will easily rid herself of me.

The extent and depth of her own bitterness frightened her. The night went on. She counted her own heart-beats and listened to the wind, and there was no comfort to be had.

'Oh Ben he is dead and laid in his grave,
Hum. Ha. Laid in his grave.'

When she was certain that dawn must be near, because
she had lain awake in that cold room for a hundred
years, she put on her stockings and, carrying her shoes,
went down through the silent house, stopping every so
often, in dread of waking them. They did not wake. In
the kitchen, she saw that it was ten to five by the clock,
but the sky was still dark. It was bitterly cold, and the
wind had risen again, a gate banged, somewhere in the
lane.

On the dresser was the parcel, wrapped in brown
paper. Alice had pointed it out to her last night. 'You
can take it with you. It all belongs to you now, doesn't
it?' and Ruth had been too dazed to follow what she
meant. Now, she touched it, and supposed that it con-
tained some old things Ben had never taken up to the
cottage, things they now wanted rid of.

For a second, she hesitated, suffused with guilt.
Perhaps she ought to write a note to them, to apolo-
gise. But what did she have to say that they would
believe? It would make no difference, things were as
they were. And she could not breathe in this house,
she wanted to shake the sight and smell of it off her for
good, to forget that she had ever been here.

She took up the parcel and opened the door, and
the wind blew hard and cold into her face, the roadway
gleamed with black ice. And then she was running

down the still-dark street, her hair was wrenched back and streaming behind her like a banner, she was stumbling and almost falling every few yards on the slippery road, but she thought of nothing except getting away, getting home. Somehow, by running, forcing herself into the wind, she might scour herself clean of yesterday. But, just outside the village, she was forced to slow down, and stop, the blood rang in her ears, her head throbbed, and she gasped and shuddered for breath.

The sky was just beginning to pale, as she walked, slowly now, for she was exhausted, up the slope leading to the common.

Here, everything looked familiar, impersonal, like the surface of the moon. There was no life. The revelation of the previous day, the sense of joy and insight and illumination, were gone, and would never return, for they had surely been delusions? She had not been in her right mind. Now, she saw the cottage and the common and the tops of the trees, and knew her world for what it was, in the stained, seeping light of dawn.

But she was home. She was grateful for that. Here, she could be herself, live or die. Do nothing. Endure.

The wind had dropped quite suddenly. She opened the back door and waited for the silence of the house to engulf her. Knew what she had to do. Now, at once, there could be no running away. She went up the stairs.

*

She had forgotten what the room looked like. It was very cold. It might have been empty for years past. She walked around it, opened the door of a wardrobe, and then a drawer, a cupboard, looking at what was there, she picked up his hairbrush and touched the bristles to her face. None of it seemed to have anything to do with her now. Then was this all? Was there nothing more to come? Was this deadness to be what she had to live with, the absence of all grief or love or fear? Nothing more?

She took off her coat and laid it on the chair. And then, because nothing was going to happen, and there seemed nothing else she had to do, she opened the brown paper parcel. She had not thought. It was so obvious and yet she had not expected it. She took them out, one by one, these clothes in which he had died, the blue shirt and the dark, woollen jersey, the corduroy trousers and thick socks, and lifted each one up, wanting to smell, beneath the wool or cotton, his own smell. She did not, and then realised that the things had been newly washed and ironed.

She put her head down and pressed her face into the pile of garments and at last the grief broke open and drowned her, for they had taken even this away from her, they had washed away his blood and now, she understood fully and finally that Ben was dead and gone from her, that she had nothing, nothing left.

4

The death of Ben Bryce had been like a stone cast into still water, and the water had become a whirlpool with Ruth sucked down into the terrible heart of it. But the waves spread out, through the countryside down to the village and beyond the village. People felt changed, as by war or earthquake or fire, even those who lived closest to death and knew its face.

And shock and grief drew them closer together, feelings were observed and understood among them, though nothing might be said. For no one could remember being so affected by any one death. Accidents happened, life was uncertain, a child or an old man or an animal was killed, new graves were dug in the churchyard often enough, there was mourning. Why was this different? What had it been about Ben Bryce? They thought of him and tried to discover, and each of them had some particular memory upon which to dwell, and the memories, taken together, revealed all the aspects of love.

Potter, in his own cottage, planned to set out the first vegetable seedlings under glass. But he did nothing, except sit, with some half-eaten bread and cheese at his hand, remembering. And his dog Teal, sensing the change in him, was restless, would not settle in front of the fire, but padded about the house, or came up to Potter and bumped its head against the man's leg for reassurance

Potter had known death. Had seen his own brother cough and choke himself dead, of a slow lung disease, had been at the bedside of his mother and his father, when death had come to them, in old age. But that had been expected, a natural thing, he would not have had them grow any older, weakening and crumbling in body and mind, suffering more. This was not the same. He could not believe that Ben Bryce was dead. Ben, who had been so vital, and contented with himself, and with the world. Those who were with him had felt his health and pleasure and confidence in living overtake them and seep into their own minds and hearts, though he had not been any saint, nor always an easy man to work with, there were times when he withdrew into himself, as though in defence, and no one could tell his thoughts, people kept at a distance from him. There were times when he spoke his mind and it was too close to the truth.

It was not only the circumstances of the accident ——h Potter could not forget, the creak and crash of tree and the silence which had followed. come over him as he bent down and nan was dead. In that moment, he had discovered some great, clear truth and that truth had changed him. Kneeling on the moist earth beside the still figure, he had felt entirely alone with death and known that it was good. If he had ever doubted immortality, he could not doubt it now. Awe had come over him, and a kind of reverence, he had knelt and been, for a while, paralysed, for the whole wood was filled with this momentous thing, this parting of body and soul. And when he had put out a hand and touched Ben Bryce's arm, felt his wrist and the thick bone, and the hairs covering the flesh, it had been like an electric shock, some impulse, whose meaning he did not fully understand, had passed into him. And it had not left him, he felt it still.

Standing at the very back of the small church during the funeral, he had known it again, though the shock of the death had come fully upon him by then, the numb sense of disbelief, and there was grief, too, for himself, for Ruth, for all of them, at this loss.

He shook his head. There had been a door through which he had passed and now, on the other side of it, he tried to come to terms with what he found, with his altered self.

He lived alone, had done so for thirty years, and he was content; he was not a thinking man. Now, he could do nothing save think.

The dog was snuffling at the crack under the door, and then it came back to Potter, whined softly, so that the man got up, they went out into the raw, grey evening. They walked down through the beech woods and Low Field, up on to the ridge, and over the other side. Nothing moved, nothing had colour, the sky looked sour.

It seemed to him that things would not be the same again, with him, or with the rest of the village, their world had tilted, and they must get accustomed to it, for there would be no going back.

He stayed out until dark, and, returning, he saw a light in Ruth Bryce's window, and paused, looking at it, distressed for her, but knowing that he could not go near, because he would be rejected, he carried upon him the taint of her husband's dying. He did not know what would happen to her. He felt fear.

In the house at Foss Lane, it was as though a dank fog had crept into every room and settled there, and all night and all day, there was the sound of Dora Bryce's weeping. She lay in bed, or else got up and sat huddled near the grate, and her eyes and lips were swollen and stained with the salt of her tears. When she spoke, it was only to herself, the same, bitter, repeated words.

'Why should it happen to me? What have I done to deserve it? What harm did he ever do? How shall I live, how shall I live? How can he be dead?'

And, after a time, it embarrassed or irritated them and they gave up trying to console or quieten her. Arthur Bryce stood about, a large man with a damaged arm and shoulder, helpless, his own grief buried far within him, never articulated; and Jo retreated, out into the woods or over beyond the ridge, walked alone, before going to Ruth, to do her work for her, and to give and receive comfort.

It was Alice who lost her temper, for she realised, now, how much she loathed this house, and wanted to be free from it, she felt stifled and unnerved in the close atmosphere of self-pity and bitterness generated by her mother, and she had nothing with which to occupy herself, nowhere to go.

In the middle of the evening, she got up suddenly, went and stood over her mother and shook her arm. Dora Bryce rocked herself to and fro, like a creature in pain.

'Stop that! Stop that, mother, how do you think we can bear to hear you, crying and crying, and complaining? Don't you think we feel, too? Don't you think all of us feel, but what good are you doing? What help is it?'

Her mother stared up at her and saw the girl's face, angry, proud and without pity.

'It does no good, does it? Will it alter things? Will it bring him back? Haven't you any dignity, any pride in yourself?'

She was disgusted, not only by the endless crying, but because her mother would not bother with herself, would not wash or brush out her hair or change her clothes, and the cooking and work about the house she left to be managed somehow, by Alice and Jo.

'What good will it do?'

Dora Bryce did not answer, only moved nearer the fire, trapped in the vicious circle of her own misery and resentment. She thought, now my own daughter is turning against me, and what have I left? A man who gives me no help, a man no use for anything, and a child who might not belong here. What have I left in this world? And she thought again of her first born, her son, Ben, and how he had been, and her imagination gilded him with every perfection, every virtue, it seemed to her, now, that he had been the only one of them to love her, that he had paid her constant attention, had cared, had understood, as none of the others wanted to understand. Ben.

The sobbing rose up from her stomach and the ugly, angry noise began again. She did not notice when Alice, too, went out, that they had all left her, because they were exhausted and ashamed, they had lost patience. She said, I have had nothing in my life, no satisfaction, no fulfilment, no rewards or pleasures, I have been cheated and deceived.

The death of her son only confirmed it, only reminded her of what she might have had, what she ought to have been.

Now, there was nothing.

The curate, Thomas Ratheman, leaned over the bed of his sleeping daughter, saw the fine, mauve-flushed skin of her closed eyelids, and felt all the old amazement, that she should have come from him, and now be here, a separate life. But he was troubled, he could not forget Ruth Bryce, who had hidden from him when he called, and the sight of her face, and the way she had carried herself, apart from everyone else, at the funeral.

He thought he should go to her again, talk, help her somehow with her grief, and though he was conscientious, he did not think to do this out of duty but for love, he had come to love all these people.

The child, Isobel, stirred, turned over and murmured in sleep and, thinking of the fallen tree, the sudden, casual death, he was afraid for her in this world, he said, nothing shall touch her, no harm shall ever come to her; even while knowing that it was not possible, not true, that she must grow and suffer and change, if she were ever to be herself and free.

Ben Bryce had left no child for his wife's comfort. Did she regret it? Again, the idea of going there, now, even so late in the evening, came to him urgently, and he knew why, remembering he had heard one or other of them say, in the village that morning:

'She'll do away with herself, she'll not bear it like this, on her own, you mind.'

He had stopped and prayed, at that moment, for Ruth to have courage and for evil not to overtake her.

When he was a boy, a friend of his father's, a priest too, had hanged himself from a roof beam in the barn, a year after his wife's death; a year during which he had fought with misery and loneliness and temptation, and had failed, had succumbed, worn out and crazed by it all.

And the same night, Ratheman's father had woken in a sweat of fear, his head full of a dream he had had, of the friend in some appalling need and distress, and he would have dressed and gone to him, although it was seven miles away and winter, thick snow. But, standing, undecided, in the bedroom, he had listened to reason which told him that a dream was a dream and not prophetic, that the fears had sprung from some dark place in his own mind. He was a reasonable man, scholarly, faithful, unimaginative, he did not set store by his own chance emotions, or those of others, and so he had gone back to bed and the dream did not disturb him again.

In the morning, very early, someone had come through the snow to tell him of his friend's suicide, in the middle of the previous night. He had never ceased to blame himself and pray for forgiveness, of God and of his friend, for the rest of his life, tormented by the dream which had been a cry for help that he had not answered. That experience, that death, had aged and altered him, and his son had not forgotten either, so that now, thinking of Ruth Bryce, he was restless and perturbed, he prayed again, and, if the child had not woken and begun to cry loudly, with some pain, he would have gone to the cottage, for his own peace of mind.

*

Rydal, in his office, lit and re-lit a pipe, used up match after match, and sought to attend to his paper work and could not, nor could he think what money he should offer to Ruth Bryce, or whether she would even accept it from him. They were his woods, it had been his tree, and so he was to blame, though they had contradicted him, Potter, and Heykes, the farm manager, they had all of them been to inspect the fallen elm and Rydal saw for himself that they could not have known, nobody could have prevented it, But at night, he lay awake, sick with guilt and with a sense of the futility of his own life, of all their lives.

Ben Bryce, who had worked for him since he was fifteen, and even before that, in summer evenings and holidays, for the pleasure of it, who had been reliable, thorough, industrious. Oh, but more than that, more, for all the men worked well enough, it was not only that. Ben Bryce. Rydal had liked to go and talk to him, say some word about the state of the trees, the weather, vermin, anything, he had liked to stand watching the young man at work, because he exuded some sort of contentment and strength, some satisfaction with the world which Rydal knew that he himself had lacked, perhaps ever since he was born. Silent Ben Bryce might sometimes have been, withdrawn, or else abruptly outspoken; but he was never dissatisfied, never unsure. He had been at one with things.

Now, packing down the dark tobacco in the pipe

bowl and lighting it again, Rydal thought, I am an old man; though he was not yet sixty. But it seemed that no blood ran in his veins, no life at all. His skin and flesh were dried out, his hair was thin, and he had no purpose, no hope. He was a rich man, and respected, the blue-bound wage book was thick with the list of men who worked for him, and none of it counted, none of it had value. He had stood in the church at Ben Bryce's funeral and thought only that life had no meaning, and his own least of all.

The pipe was dead again, the taste of burnt smoke bitter in his mouth. He looked down at the papers and did not know, still, about the money for Ruth Bryce and had no heart to work, nor to go back into the huge house and sit opposite the wife who did not love him.

Instead, he walked as far as the top gate, and, leaning on it, looked over the land which belonged to him, and he would have given away all of it, in reparation, because it brought him no joy, and because the tree which had killed Ben Bryce had been his tree and the guilt would never leave him.

No one could have told how old Moony knew, how the ripples had spread out to where he lived, six miles from the village, or whether he had picked the news up somewhere, on his endless walking, nor could they guess that he, too, was, in his own way, affected.

Years ago, his place had been a hut for shepherds, forced to spend nights out during lambing time or in bad weather, there was only one room and the stone walls were patched up with old corrugated tin sheeting, the roof hung askew and leaked at the corner, so that inside, there was always the smell of damp and, often, a pool of water on the floor. But Moony was never cold, never ill. He had a fire, logs or brushwood or peat, and as often as not, the smoke blew back down the chimney tunnel, and clung to the walls, there was a crust of soot over them.

He had carried the news of Ben Bryce's death back, and brooded over it now, in the reeking hut. He knew them all by name, though they never spoke, but something had set Ben Bryce apart from the rest, and his young brother the same. They told the truth.

In one corner, a tame raven with a damaged wing and no name perched like a scarecrow, and, as Moony fed it out of his hand with bits of bread and grain, he turned over in his mind what he had learned about death. Others might think it chance, or a cruel blow of fate, others might think there were dozens, older, weaker, less good, who should have been struck down before him. But others were wrong. It seemed to Moony that when a man was ready for death, fitted to it, then death did well to take him, before he was altered and soiled by all the evil in this world.

'I'm ready,' he said, as the bird jabbed its hard, bright beak down to the palm of his hand. 'I've been ready time enough.' And so had Ben Bryce, there had been a look about his eyes, the settled look of a man who knew himself and this world, and so, was ready to leave them.

So Moony thought, and more, cooking up his can of meat – a grouse, poached from under one of Rydal's hedges. He used to tell himself that, one day, he would write it all down, one day – but now he knew that was not necessary, his thoughts were what he lived by, and they were too rich and deep for others. The plans he made, the questions he asked and answered were to his own satisfaction, and that was enough. He lived within himself, as within the four walls of the hut, and had not expected to be moved or startled by anything outside.

Now, this, and it was no ordinary death.

The raven fluffed out its feathers, and then settled down again into them, half-closed its eyes, so that, as it grew dark, there was only the sullen burning of the fire.

The pool was unsettled for a long time, they none of them could feel that life would return to normal, everyone still spoke or brooded, or, like Dora Bryce, moaned and wept, about the death, and perhaps the children were affected more than any, sensing uncertainty and danger, so that, in this house and that, all about the countryside, there were bad dreams and eyes wide open in fear, there was restlessness and bewilderment.

That first week of March blew itself out in gales and rainstorms, Lent came in but the Spring might never follow.

5

She thought, how can I go on crying, for there can be no tears left in me? But it was a bottomless well. And there were so many kinds of weeping; the harsh, raking sobs and then a silent steady flow, as she lay inert upon the bed. Her face was sore and chapped and sometimes she got up and bathed it in cold water and was soothed. But she no longer cared to look at herself in the glass, for the tears had made her ugly, Ben would have been ashamed of her. Quite often, this thought came, and she could imagine his voice in the room, begging her to stop, because her crying distressed him, he said, 'Don't cry for me. Why? Why? All's well with me. It's done with, over, and now, nothing can hurt me again.'

And this made her angry, she screamed back at him, told him the truth, that she was crying for herself, for her own loss, and her dread of the empty future, not for him, not for him. How could he not understand? She blamed him for leaving her, said, you have everything and I have nothing, At least let me do this, leave me alone to weep.

Days passed and nights passed and, sometimes, Jo was there, and she did not care if he heard her or saw her face. Time was not measured out in hours or by lightness and dark, grief had a time of its own, and a rhythm, so that she was either weeping over some particular memory, or craving for his physical body and its closeness, like a child taken from its mother; or else her mind was a blur, like the windows that streamed with rain, she was drowning, but never quite losing consciousness in it all. But she did know, in some way, when it was evening, and time to put the hens into their coop and then, no matter how she felt, she always got up and stumbled down through the wet garden, she did not miss a day.

At times, she woke up, cramped with cold, but unable to make the effort of pulling blankets over her, or going down to the fire Jo always made up. Or else she was thirsty, with the kind of desperate thirst which seemed to reach down to the pit of her stomach, which was shrivelled and burning. She got up and drank water from a white jug, pint after pint, it hurt her throat to swallow, but still the thirst was not slaked. She did eat, picked up a piece of fruit or a raw vegetable, some cheese, and crammed it into her mouth, because it seemed to be in some way obscene, the act of eating was ugly, inhuman.

She slept, by day or by night, for hours or minutes, and sometimes dreamed, of Jo's leering, threatening tree-faces. But it still seemed that this was a time to endure, a grief to pass through, like a dark tunnel, and at the end of it, everything would be as it had always been, she would be with Ben again. She thought, dying is like being born, and now I am doing both, with Ben. For she wanted to share in everything with him, could not accept that, in death, he had to be alone. She said, I should have been with him, I wanted to have been there with him when the tree fell, there when he died, I failed him, I left him by himself.

But out of it all, two days separated themselves, two days in which everything changed and she was temporarily released from weeping and restored to herself, sane and quieted.

The first time, Jo was there, down in the kitchen, and she in bed, and exhausted beyond bearing with grief, and for a while, she had no more tears left, she slept, for how long she could not tell, but it was like a waking sleep, a trance, and in it, she dreamed of Ben. He was here, in the room with her, but he would not let her see his face, he stood somewhere just behind her. She sensed that he did not want her to turn round; but he was Ben, real and whole and unharmed, and more alive, more himself than he had ever been, so that she was startled, she thought, or said, 'I never knew I had so much, I thought you were ... but I didn't know anything about you, you were a shadow then, but now ... and I never knew.'

It did not distress her. How could it? When he was so much more, so fulfilled and perfected?

For a while, nothing else happened, in the dream, except this awareness and the fact that she was not allowed to see him.

And then he said, 'I will always help you.'

'Yes.'

'Wherever you are, I will always help you. Ruth?'

'Yes.'

'Ruth…'

She was coming awake to the sound of her own name, lying very quietly on the bed. She and the room and the whole house were filled with the dream. But something else, also. Outside, the sky was mould-grey, it was late afternoon, raining. But Ruth saw, instead, the other light, glowing out of everything and it was the same light that had changed the face of the world on the day before Ben's dying, and at the funeral.

The chair beside the bed, and the faded floral curtains, the dark oak wardrobe and the mirror and the ceiling were lit from within, as though some fire were burning deep down, but it was not a harsh, bright light, it was pale and translucent. And Ruth herself seemed to be filled with it. She lifted up her arm and saw each finger and the milky nails and blue veins, the joint of her wrist, as though they were newly made, and of some substance altogether finer and more beautiful than flesh and bone. She closed her eyes and opened them again, but it was still the same. Except that, as the sky outside darkened, the light in the room glowed more strongly. She lay and let it bathe over her like spring-water, she felt entirely calm, rested and refreshed. All the crying was done with, that had belonged to another time and place, a different Ruth.

She remembered the words and spoke them aloud.

'And he will wipe every tear from their eyes and death shall be no more. Neither shall there be mourning nor crying nor pain any more, for the former things have passed away.'

So now she knew, she understood, as she understood only that in the church. She wept, not tears of relief but of gratitude.

Jo knocked quietly on the door, and when she answered, came in, and stopped, a little way from the bed.

'Jo?'

It was dark. The dream and the light were fading.

'What is it?'

She heard her own voice and it sounded as it used to sound. She turned her head. There was a curious, puzzled or frightened expression on his face. He came slowly over to her, knelt down and put his head on her arm.

'What happened, Ruth? Something happened.'

'It's all right.'

'What happened? I was in the kitchen and … I don't know what it was.'

'You shouldn't be afraid, Jo.'

'I don't know.'

'It wasn't anything bad.'

'*What* was it, Ruth?'

She was silent. The room had gone quite dark, now. She was fully awake.

She said, 'I don't know what it was.' Because that was the truth.

'Do you feel better?'

'Yes. I went to sleep.'

She put her hand out and touched his head. The hair was thick and coarse-textured. Not like Ben's. He had thought or felt something, the dream had passed through him, too, but not for long enough, and he was afraid. She wondered if she might come to be so, too, and remembered what had happened before, that she had forgotten the dream entirely and tried to recall it – and failed. That would be so again, and then the world would be unbearably real, dead and opaque and colourless. Perhaps it might come back. But only if she did not ask or expect it. And if it did not? If it had never been?

No, it had been. And if it was only a dream, then wasn't that something, a lull, a peace at the heart of the storm? She might always sleep and dream again.

She got up and went to put away the hens, and then stood for a moment or two, her ankles deep in the wet grass, stroking the nose and neck of the donkey, and everything was quiet, and she was quiet within herself.

*

That night, and the day following it, were worse than any she had lived through before. Jo went home. She poured out a cup of milk and began to sip it, and heard the rain pattering off the roof on to the grass. And she was ice-cold, her flesh felt stiff, the roof of her mouth was dry. She thought, Ben is dead and in his grave, and that is all, he is nowhere, there is nothing left of him and so it would have been better if he had not lived. There was no point in my meeting and loving and marrying him, no purpose in our happiness. For there is only this world and the misery of it, there was a chance, an accident, the falling of a tree and the person who was Ben, thinking and feeling, the live person, was finished, gone into a black pit, he knew nothing about it, and he knows nothing now. He is nowhere. He should never have been, the whole world should never have been.

She was sick with dread that this was the truth, now that she was wide awake, and that the dream was nothing, as the light had been nothing, or else some illusion she had somehow manufactured for her own consolation, her own deception. She cried out, 'Why did you give it to me, if you were going to take it away? Why did you give me Ben and then kill him?' And did not know who she was accusing, God or not-God, life or death, or Ben himself.

She was certain, then, that her mind was diseased and her feelings delusions, that she was mad to believe what she had believed. She leaned over the wooden table and wept and cried out like an animal in a trap, words and non-words, all caught up and whirled about anyhow among the tears. She wiped her arm over her face again and again, and then, because she wanted to escape, somehow, somehow, she went to the wall and beat her head against it, and then her fists, and when she felt pain, only beat harder, for the one thing she had left was the power to injure herself, as Ben had been injured.

She did not go back upstairs, there was no strength in her, she lay on the floor in front of the fire and sobbed there, her face pressed into the rug, and all night, the rain, the rain.

Once, half-waking, she wished that her Godmother Fry were still alive, for she was the only person who might have helped her. Godmother Fry had believed, had talked to Ruth once, and without dread, about her own death, which would surely come soon, for she was almost ninety; she had been ready, she trusted. Everything Ruth believed had come from Godmother Fry, or from Ben, for they had been alike, in the things they knew, which were not of this world. It had been her Godmother who taught her that Easter was the time which counted, the testing time, for Christmas was tinselled over with legend and children's dreams, it was true, but Easter was stripped bare of the dreams, Easter was suffering and death and resurrection, was despair and hope and certainty.

And Easter was not long away, and she could not tell if it would matter to her now.

Early in the morning, she came out of some half-sleep, half-death, aching and shivering with cold and exhaustion, but still she could not move, she lay all through the morning, her eyes open, staring at the dead ashes in the grate, and she had never known, until now, what it was truly to despair.

Jo came. Saw her. Knelt down and touched her. She said nothing. He left her, she heard him doing the jobs he always did, and she thought dimly that she should get up, because he, too, needed help, love, and perhaps she frightened or disgusted him.

She closed her eyes again to shut out the dank, grubby daylight, and the sight of the cold ashes, and put her hands up to her ears to muffle the sound of the endless rain. And through her head, the same words. He is dead. He is nothing. He is nowhere. He is dead. He is dead. She made clutching movements with her fists, as if she could somehow take hold again of her old belief or hope, but there was only the empty air.

She did get up, though there seemed no reason for it, and washed herself and her hair, and stared at the water coming from the tap – water, which she had always thought beautiful, in its clearness and suppleness, any water, sea or stream, rain or pond; and now it was like everything else, dead, and when it dribbled away, dirtied by its contact with her own skin and hair, she was repelled by it.

*

In the kitchen, Jo stood beside the range, feeling the heat coming off it, but it did not warm him, he shivered because he was so afraid for Ruth, he so loved her, and was helpless, there was nothing he could do or say, no way he could reach her. No one else could share this with him. At Foss Lane, her name was never spoken, and his mother, her own crying ended now, dragged herself about the house, an old woman, his father came and went to work, ate and drank, said nothing,

What should he do?

'God,' he said, 'God, please ...'

What? He was not sure. 'Make her well again. Make her well.' But in his heart he thought that nothing could make her well, except Ben, the old life.

He saw the rose-quartz, still on the table, and touched it and felt, as when he first saw it, some kind of truth which emanated from the crystal and was bound up with the shaping of it. Then, he could not believe in death. He knew that it was not so, had always known. But how to tell Ruth? How to make her believe it? He had thought that she did. Yesterday, when there had been such a stillness and peace in the house, and in her, her voice and touch, yesterday, relief had spurted up within him, because she was well again, she knew, something had happened.

And now, today …

He put the kettle on the range and boiled it and made tea, cupping his hands around the china and holding it close to his face for warmth. He heard the door of the bedroom close and dare not go up to her with a drink, because somehow, her fear and despair and misery might reach out and enter him, eat away at his own strength and belief.

And so, he tidied up and put some food on a covered plate, and a note on the kitchen table, and left, to walk, in the rain across the fields and over the ridge, where he could breathe again, take hold of himself, where all the fear and unhappiness drained out of him. Because always, here, he sensed that Ben was with him, and be was healed by the contact.

He prayed, looking over the misty fields and black wet woods, that his deepest fear of all would not come true. That Ruth would not kill herself.

*

She asked for nothing, expected nothing. And so, this second day came to her as a gift, and she was startled out of her-self, but accepted it gladly, and it shone out ever afterwards, like some golden coin lying among dull pebbles.

The sun woke her, it filled the room, and was

bright on her face and her arms, stretched above her head, and when she went to the window, she saw a shimmering blue sky and the last of the raindrops like baubles of glass on the hedge. Aconites and snowdrops were clustered here and there under the bushes.

She had an overwhelming desire to get away from here, to slough off all the days and nights of weeping and the memories of death. She washed and dressed, and felt an odd excitement, like a tingling under the skin.

Jo was walking up the garden with the scoop full of eggs, and when she called to him, he hesitated, anxious, for they had scarcely spoken these last days, he had come and gone like a shadow. And now, she stood in the doorway in a fresh blue dress, her face changed, softened.

'Happy,' Jo thought, 'she looks happy.' And he wanted to cry with relief, for she was Ruth again, the Ruth he knew, he could reach her. She had not killed herself. Every morning, be had dreaded reaching the house, for fear of what he might find there.

'Twelve eggs,' he said, 'two of the hens are broody, I think.'

'Jo ...' But she did not know how to tell him of what she felt, how to thank him for having come here so faithfully and done the work and asked no questions, never tried to intrude. She loved him now, as she loved no one else in the world.

He held the eggs out to her.

'Jo, let's go somewhere.'

He frowned.

'I don't want to be here, not today, I'm so tired of it – upstairs – all the rain. But I woke up and saw the sun – I want to go out.'

'It's the market at Thefton.'

'Oh no.'

No, not there. For what she wanted was not to remember, not to have any of the past thrown up before her eyes, but to forget, just for this one day, to get away, somewhere else, somewhere new. She knew that this was a day which would not come again, that the grieving was not over but only suspended in time, so that she might take a breath, recover something of herself.

'Jo, we'll go ...'

She hesitated. Everywhere about this countryside, all the fields and woods and valleys, even as far as the river, held memories, were too close.

'We'll go to the sea.'

'The sea?' He sounded unsure.

'On the train. We can walk to Thefton. And have a whole day – at Hadwell Bay.'

'That's where we went for our holiday. Where I found the stones. Hadwell Bay !'

It was still early, seven o'clock, there would be a train sometime that morning.

'Ruth ...'

They had gone into the sun-filled kitchen. Jo was putting the eggs away. She turned.

'I was afraid... I was afraid you'd never be well.'

'Jo ... Oh, I'm sorry, I didn't think of you. You come up here every day and I don't talk to you, I ...'

'No, it was ...' He shook his head.

'A dream?'

'No.'

"What is it?'

'Sometimes, in the night, the house is so quiet. And they don't know if I'm there or not. They don't know anything. Then, I think about you.'

'Do you think about Ben? Do you miss him?'

'I – it's strange.'

'How?'

'I go over there, up on the ridge and then I see – then I think about him. Over there. It's all right. I know it is. Ben was different. He wasn't like us.'

'Yes. He was like you.'

'When I was seven, I killed a rabbit. There was a boy I knew – he lived at Hedgely – and he borrowed his father's gun – or took it. He said he knew how to shoot and I didn't. I never would. It made me angry. I said I could, I could do anything he did, anything in the world. So I had to show him, and he gave me the gun. It was very heavy. I didn't think guns were so heavy. It hurt my arm. But I saw a rabbit – it wasn't very far away and it didn't move. And I shot it. I heard it squeal, I ... And that was the only truly wicked thing

I've ever done in my life. I can remember it – the sound it made. And it was my fault.'

He was standing a few feet away from her, holding himself stiffly.

'I cried in the night,' he said, 'I couldn't stop hearing it. I dreamed about it. Ben came. I told Ben. I've never told anyone else.'

There was nothing she could say, but she realised then as never before how close he had been to his brother, how much Ben's death had affected him.

The kitchen was warm, it smelled of something fresh, clean. She looked around her and saw how tidy Jo had made it, how he had arranged the pans and dishes on the shelves, and polished the top of the range until it shone. What would she have done, how could she have lived, without Jo?

She said, 'Shall we go to the sea?'

'If – I'll do what you want.'

He searched her face and saw her excitement, her hope of pleasure, said, 'Yes. We'll go.' And abruptly, he came and put his arms round her, she heard him say, 'The sea!' and his voice was full of wonder.

The sun rose higher and shone like a disc of metal out of a transparent sky.

They might have been the only people in the world. Hadwell Bay curved out in front of them, the sea far, far out, the sand flat and pale and, closer to them, the rocks glistening wet, with small, secret pools hidden in their clefts, as though cupped between two hands. It was very still, quite warm and at the rim of the horizon, the sky was silver-white.

Jo stood, looking, as if he could not believe in any of it.

He said, 'It's the same. It smells the same ... it's ...' He pressed his arms to his sides tightly, and released them again.

'What can we do?'

'Anything. You say.'

Already, for Ruth, the day had taken on the quality of a dream, she was in it and yet outside of it, but whatever happened, she must hold hard on to every moment, nothing must slip past her unnoticed.

They walked very slowly down on to the beach and the sand made a rasping sound as they stepped on it, the imprints of their feet strung out behind them, like small, following animals. There was no wind, but everywhere, a particular smell of salt and fish and the curious reek of the black ribbon seaweed, scattered with small blisters, which Jo went for, and carried over his arm.

'If you take it and hang it outside the door, you can tell the weather – if it's going to be wet or dry, by how the seaweed feels in your hand.'

And then he left her again, to climb over some pinkish brown rocks. A different weed was draped over them like green hair, slimy to touch.

'Sea anemones,' he called, and she followed him, they bent down together and saw their own two faces reflected in the rock pool, their eyes dark and shining in pale moons. And again, breathing up the sea smell, she thought, I shall never forget this, and I shall never come here again, in case it is spoiled, changed. She put her finger down into the cold water and touched a fronded anemone and it closed over the tip like the pink wet mouth of an infant suckling a nipple.

'They're alive,' Jo said, 'they're not just plants, they're really a kind of animal.'

He was happy, released from the anxiety and strain of the past days. Looking at him, Ruth thought that if she had done nothing else, at least she had given him this.

They walked and walked along the rim of the sea, which only shifted a little, and the sun shone on to them and on to the cliffs above them, the sky was spread thin as new paint, Jo found shells, razors and conches and an abalone, and very small, smooth pink pebbles, and stored them all away in his pockets. She did not wish for Ben to be here, it was enough that she had Jo, they were held together in this capsule of quiet, sunlit pleasure.

They lay on the sand, and Ruth half closed her eyes, so that the sea and sky danced together, were incandescent, it was a magic world and time went on forever.

*

It was dark, and much colder. Coming up the lane, her body seemed to be floating and her head was full of the sound of the waves, she felt washed clean by the salt air and sunlight, the reflections off the water. She was vividly awake, every nerve was vibrating, she heard every sound very clearly, like the ringing of bells; their own footsteps on the road, the creak of a tree branch, the quick dart of some animal in the ditch. When she breathed, it was as though the fresh air passed through every vein.

The moon was full, papery pale as a circle of honesty.

Jo was tired and silent, hugging the brightness and joy of the day close to himself. At the bottom of the slope, they stopped. He should turn right to the village, and Ruth would go on, up to the common. But perhaps she should go with him to Foss Lane, perhaps, in this mood, she would be able to say something to them, break through the barriers of hostility and mistrust.

'They don't know where you've been. I ought to come with you, tell them.'

'They don't care.'

'But...'

'Nobody notices. Don't come, Ruth, don't.'

His voice was tense.

'I ought to talk to them.'

'No. And I don't want them to know anything about today. It's private, I don't want it to be spoiled and if they know, it will be. Don't come.'

She sensed that he was trying to protect her from them and that there were other, hidden reasons of his own.

'I'll come tomorrow.'

He turned away from her, then back again, he hugged her tightly for a second. He said, 'Thank you, thank you,' and reached into his pocket, took out one of the shells, the abalone, and gave it to her.

'Jo – don't forget today. Don't forget anything about it.'

But she had no need of a reply.

He walked off and she stayed there, holding the shell, listening to his footsteps, and did not want to go back to the cottage, because once there she would know that the day was over, and that what she had deliberately put out of her mind would be waiting for her in the empty rooms. And a sudden picture of Ben, walking towards her across the common, filled her head and she cried out, because he was not there, because she was alone in the dark lane, she wanted to be with him and there was no way, no way.

There was a way.

As she came to the top of the hill, she began to run, as though time mattered and she might somehow be too late, might find him gone. And she blamed herself for having stayed away so long, she had to make up for all the days and nights of neglect.

She had imagined him to be with her, in the cottage or else gone somewhere beyond her reach, but now, she faced what seemed to be the only truth, that this was where they had brought, and left him. Had others been here? Had Dora Bryce and Alice and the black mourners, the neighbours and relatives? If they had, she resented it, she wished this to be a private place, a locked garden to which only she had the key. But it was open, anyone might walk in and view, as they had all stared down upon him in the open coffin.

She walked through the lych-gate and then stepped on to the grass, moving between the old, moss-covered headstones. The flints on the church face gleamed pewter. She did not need the moonlight, she could have found her way unerringly if she had been blind.

The old graves gave way to new, along the south side of the church, with his the last, the most recent, at the end, and beyond that, open grass.

Ruth stopped dead. They had taken the flowers away, all of them, there was only a bare oblong mound, like a molehill pushed up through the turf. It might have belonged to any one, any stranger. She could not register the truth of where she was and what it meant, it did not seem possible Ben here, Ben dead, and never able to speak or move or breathe again in this world. It was a nonsense.

She knelt down on the grass. She said, 'We went to the sea, Jo and I. To Hadwell Bay. And there was only the sand and the sky and the sunlight, we walked and walked. You should have been there. Why weren't you there, why?'

Silence pressed in upon her. The yew trees and the poplars were columns of stone.

She thought, what has happened to him now, what does he look like, how has he changed? She did not know anything about the time it all took. And in a moment of terror and desire to rescue him, to free him from the prison of earth and the pale wooden box and bring him back to life, she scrabbled at the turf and tore it and a lump came away easily in her hand, for it was loosely laid, there had not been time for it to take root. She let it drop and her hands were mealy with the crumbs of soil.

Then a picture came before her eyes of his body lying in that close darkness, straight and still, and of his flesh beginning to flake and fall away from the bones, his hair drying and going brittle and the blood caking inside his veins. She told herself, over and over again, what she knew when she was sane m her mind, she said, what is here is nothing, this is not Ben, this is an old coat, like a chrysalis, outgrown and of no more use, he is not here. Then where, where? For the flesh she had loved and the breath which had mingled with her own breathing, all she had been able to see and hear and touch of Ben, were under her feet, the same – and no longer the same, nothing.

If she had been afraid of how the tree had injured his body, what was that? That was nothing to what the earth and the creatures and the juices of the earth were doing now, to how they would break down and utterly destroy him.

Words, phrases reeled through her head, one detached itself and she spoke it aloud.

'A time to be born and a time to die,' and she believed that to be true. But if she had known when she first met Ben that his time to die would so soon come, she would have gone away from him at once, would never have taken the appalling risk of love.

Would she?

But she did not know, she knew nothing any more.

She was beyond tears, and so she lay down on the mound of turf and rested, hoping, hoping, and the hours passed, the moon rose, and she was given nothing, no comfort, there was only the chill from the ground, a seeping moisture of earth and grass. She no longer blamed anyone, God or life, Ben or chance, the falling tree. It had happened, it had been necessary, the pattern was complete. But she cried out, 'Please, please ...' without knowing for what she asked.

If she could die, herself, here, now ... But she could not.

She stayed and the warmth and brightness of sun and sea, the peace of that day, belonged to some other life, long past.

After that night, for weeks, she came here, to sit or lie beside the grave and her visits were noted, she

was watched and the story spread through the village
and out into the countryside, they talked about her.
Predicted. Waited.

6

'The sea? What are you talking about? You've gone daft, boy. The sea?'

Jo stood at the far end of the room. That night, they had been waiting up for him and in the end, he had had to give away his secret, because for some odd reason, his mother had demanded to know about his doings, though she had not noticed, until now, whether he existed or not.

'You're to tell me what you've been at.'

'We went to the sea. On the train from Thefton. That's all.'

'She may be half-crazed but does she have to drag you down in it?'

'Don't talk about Ruth like that.'

'That's it, turn against me, you as well. All of you. It's only what I've come to expect, though God knows why I should deserve it. I've tried, I've struggled on in this place and do you think this is all I was born for? Don't you think I had chances enough, when I was your age, for something better?'

The same things, over and over again. Alice sat stiffly, her face expressionless.

'How much do any of you care or understand? What do you know about how I suffer? The sacrifices I've made. You don't, you know nothing. He was the only one, he was sensitive, and he was taken from me, and what have I left?'

Jo turned one of the small stones about between his finger and thumb.

'And why does she have to have you? Going all the way up there, doing everything for her. What do you ever do for me? Why can't she lift a finger? Others have had to. Hasn't anyone told her, life goes on and she's no exception? As if I couldn't have taken to my bed and never got up. She's not in her right mind and whose fault is it but her own? She's making use of you. It's to stop. You're not to go over there, spending half the day and night, locked up with a mad woman.'

'She is not mad, you shouldn't say those things.'

'Is that how you'd talk to me? My own son? Don't you take on her airs. She's the proud one, she's cut herself off. Well then, let her be, she's nothing to us now.'

'She is to me.'

'Yes, you're on her side, she's turned you against me. How do you know anything, boy? You can't see the truth about her, a child like you. Nor he. She took him and now she's trying to take you.'

'She needs someone. Me. I have to help her.'

'Have to? And if I say you don't?' Dora Bryce turned away, making for the kitchen. 'The sea. What right has she to go spending money, going on pleasure trips, enjoying herself. The sea! So much for what she feels. How long is it? Four weeks? Less. And she can go off to the sea. She's hard as hard,'

'No,' said Jo quietly. He felt sick inside himself, but he would not let Ruth down, he would defend her against all of them.

'And what will happen to her? I'll tell you. It's only what anyone could tell you. She'll either go out of her mind and have to be taken away, or else find another man, quick enough, and be off. That's what.'

It was Alice who interrupted, Alice, not Jo, who could no longer sit in that stifling room, hearing the endless complaints, the self-pity and bitterness. She got up.

'Leave it,' she said, 'leave him alone. Does it matter where he went? It does no harm. Can't we talk like normal people, can't anybody forget about it for a moment?'

'You? You as well? Taking her side, going against me?'

'No one's against you.'

'I could have been Someone, Miss, had a real life, I could.'

'We all know what you fancy you could have been. A lady! We've heard it all our lives and do you suppose we believe it? Why should we? And does it matter? Because whatever you might have been is a day-dream, isn't it, an escape from the truth? You live in a day dream. But this is real, this is what you are, here, a woman of fifty, married to a farm hand. Well why can't you be satisfied, why not make do?'

Dora Bryce leaned against the wall, swaying slightly, a hand up to her face.

'And I'm not staying. I'm not sitting here in this room, waiting for something you dream about, hopes, half-plans, waiting this year, next year, sometime, never, and most likely it'll be never, I'm not going to be what you think you'll make of me, do what you fancy you could have done, I'll find something of my own, live my own life and be glad of it, whatever it is. I'll make do when you can't.'

Jo wanted to make them stop somehow, he could not bear the sound of their voices, raised, harsh, and the cruel words that darted to and fro and were meant to wound and to be remembered. But he could do nothing. They did not notice when he slipped out of the room and the front door, his visit to the sea was forgotten now. He went down the lane and out of the village, and the lump in his chest was waiting to rise up, he would cry, for the hatred in Foss Lane, and for what they had said about Ruth, he would cry because, if Ben had been here, he would have known what to do to silence them, to resolve everything.

He went his usual way, up the field and over the ridge, and it was not until he got there that he could let go, lie on the ground and weep. But not for himself. He would survive. It was for them, and because the memory of that magic day by the sea had been soiled over, now that they knew of it. He only had the pebbles, and be took one of them out of his pocket and held it against his face. It was something.

Alice Bryce went too, out of the cottage and, after a moment's thought, away, in a different direction, to Harmer's Barn, where Rob Foley lived. Rob Foley, the farrier, who spoke to her when he could, looked at her in a particular way. Wanted her. She felt guilty and excited and half-afraid, she felt mistress of herself, and held her head up, not caring who saw her or what they said.

And so it was Arthur Bryce, come home after drinking beer, who had to face the bitter complaints and renewed crying, on his own, and be blamed for everything that had gone wrong in her life. He sat wearily, feeling the old pain in his injured arm and shoulder, saying nothing, for where would be the point? But he wished he could have done something to make her happier, to change her life or else resign her to this one, for in spite of it all, he loved her.

*

If she had to go, again and again, to the graveyard, as though pulled by some force outside herself, there was another place, Helm Bottom, and that was different, it soothed her, all the thoughts and feelings which churned about inside her when she sat by the grave were stilled, she could take hold of herself again, here in the woods, and breathe quietly, memories came back and they were happy.

For some days, the fine, clear weather went on and there was again a sense of the approaching spring. It was early afternoon, a Saturday. She had crossed the field and gone between the beeches and the sunlight shafted in, here and there, picking out the brown and yellow of the dead leaves and gilding them, casting long, rippling shadows. She came to the bottom of the slope, in among the bushes, and then she heard it. Stopped. There was a sound of singing, coming from somewhere on the other side of the clearing, a curious chant, and the voices were high, childish. At first, she could not make out any words, nor could she see them, but after a few moments, they emerged from between the trees, in a small, slow procession. She backed a little, behind an oak tree, waited.

There were five children, girls, and she knew them all, they came from the village. Each of them wore long clothes, old skirts and dresses which belonged to their mothers or adult sisters, made of cotton or silk, and with a piece of white cloth, sheeting or curtaining, draped over their heads like nuns' veiling. The first child carried something in her hands, holding it a little away from her body, some sort of small, white box.

They seemed quite unreal, figures out of a dream or a haunting, but the sight of them stirred a memory in Ruth of the file of mourners, walking up the church path behind the coffin-bearers. Except that they had been black, all black, and the children wore white. They were singing the same lines over and over again, and none of their voices quite kept in time with one another, they did not blend.

'All the birds in the trees
Fell a-sighing and a-sobbing
When they heard of the death
Of poor Cock Robin,
When they heard of the death
Of poor Cock Robin.'

They came nearer, the singing continued without a break. They stopped, not far from the fallen elm tree, and only then, one by one, faltered into silence. The girl, Jenny Colt, who carried the box, bent down, set it on a pile of leaves, and a second child came forward and began to dig a hole with a rusty garden trowel. The others watched, their faces old-young and very solemn, their bodies like statues, draped in the long, rag-bag clothes.

The hole was made.

'Now you sing. When I bury it I say the words and you sing.'

She knelt and lifted the box, and laid it with great care in the earth, and began to say something as she covered it over with soil and leaf mould, the chanting started up again, and her own words were for a moment confused with the singing. But eventually, Ruth could make it out.

'Ashes to ashes, dust to dust, ashes to ashes, dust to dust, ashes to ashes, dust to dust, ashes to ashes, dust to dust...'

No more.

'All the birds in the trees,
Fell a-sighing and a-sobbing ...'

She had stuck a cross made of twigs into the ground, and now, got up and stood, head bowed, reverent as a priest, and the singing never stopped. Soon, they all turned and went away with the same slow steps, through the trees and their voices came floating back, until there was only the echo of them. And then silence, and the fresh grave, of some bird or small animal.

Ruth went over to the elm tree, and as she sat on it, the sun broke through here too, and she felt a moment of happiness, and more, an assurance that she would survive; she would one day emerge from the long, dark tunnel and on the other side of it, would be more herself than she had ever been, remade, whole. How it would happen or when, and what else had to come before it, she could not tell, and if she asked, would receive no answer. But if she were to drown and die, before she was allowed to live again, she would not be alone, not be without love and protection, for all she might feel that it were so.

The children were safe, because they had been able to act out the ritual of a death and a funeral, they would not come to harm. She was glad that she had seen them, and heard the solemn, broken singing, the tune and the words rang round her head for days afterwards, and at night the white figures crossed and re-crossed the paths of her dreams.

She did not go so often to the graveyard. Something else was over. She came instead to Helm Bottom and sat on the tree, remembered. For only by remembering might she piece the pattern together and understand it. Until now, she had only seen it in flashes, as though a light had been turned on to a picture, but turned off again, at once, before she had had a clear view of it.

7

For two hours each afternoon, Godmother Fry used to sleep, on the low couch in her sitting room, and then Ruth had gone out alone, to explore all of this new countryside which pleased her, because it was so unlike home. At home, the fields were flat and often, in spring or winter, colourless under water or ice; there were few trees and only thin, streaky hedges, and the sky seemed to be not only above but on all sides, like a great, bleak dome.

Here, everything had shape, and so many contrasts, in the dips and rises, the high narrow ridge and the secret pockets of woodland, here, hedges were tall, with steep, grassy banks leading up to them, and when you came to a gap or a gateway, you looked over pastures or thick corn, towards the beech woods on the far slope, or else further, to the smoky, lilac hills.

It was June. Hot. But the trees were still a fresh, sappy green, and the hay was full of clover. Traveller's joy and the white, bell flowers of convolvulus were thrown over all the hedges and trailed down like ragged clothes set out to dry, the fields were set about with ox-eye daisies and corn-marigold. Every day, Ruth picked handfuls of different flowers, white and mauve and butter yellow, and carried them back for her Godmother, and could never accept that wild plants would not thrive indoors, she arranged them faithfully, in bowls and jugs of water, only to find them the next morning, drooping and crumpled, for lack of something vital to them. But still she picked them, went scrambling up the banks, for white mouse-ear and the hidden beautiful heart's-ease, tangling her skirt in the thorn hedges and slipping, now and then, down into some dry ditch, covered over by the long grass.

She walked and walked, under the speedwell-blue sky, and everything was amazing, rare, she had never been so happy, and there was something more, just below the surface of things, some expectancy. She was nineteen, she was free, and she remembered again and again, like touching wood, that her father had married Ellen, after all the years during which he had clung on to Ruth, through anxiety and loneliness, stifling her and chaining her down, and all the time calling it love. And so it was, a kind of love, but not a good kind. If he had not married Ellen, she wondered what she would have done, how tried to break away, for she was not resourceful, or courageous.

But it was all right, it was all right. And so, she crossed fields and went along the river bank, she lay on the short, dry grass of the ridge and heard the larks which spiralled up and above her head, and was, at last, alive, a person and full of hope.

If the early afternoon sun was too hot, she walked in the woods, feeling like some sea-creature in the watery green light.

And this Friday, when she saw Ben in the clearing, at the heart of Ditcher's Copse, she realised that he was the one who had watched her as she came out of the church that Sunday, and whose face she had remembered, without knowing why.

He was sitting on the ground, with a lunch bag open beside him, and she hesitated, afraid perhaps, though not of him. He turned round hearing her.

Now, it was this sight of him which came back to her most clearly. In her memories of him in other places, later on, even when she had been closest to him, she could not recall his face, she woke in terror at night, trying and trying to bring it into view, but it was always a blur, so familiar and yet apparently already forgotten.

But this was never forgotten.

For her own part, she had never been surprised at what happened. She was only nineteen, she had known no men, outside of the circle of her father's friends and relatives, because he had discouraged any others, seeing them as threats to himself.

Here, she was newly set free, given full possession of herself for the first time in her life. And so, meeting Ben, she loved him. She was grateful that it had been

Ben, because she had been so open to love and might have met anyone and been made unhappy, and would not have been able to defend herself against it.

But it was Ben's love for her, just as immediate, which never ceased to surprise her, because he was older, twenty-seven, an independent man, he must have known others, and she did not set any particular store by herself. Her father had once said, 'You'll never make a beauty,' and she had accepted that. When she asked him, Ben had said no, there had never been anyone he wanted to know well, until now.

'You were waiting?'

'Yes. It's best to wait.'

Their first conversation she remembered so well because she had gone over it for hours in her room at Godmother Fry's that night, and all the following days, it was like a poem learned by heart in childhood, and so it came back to her easily, she could hear their voices in her head, and smell the woodland smell around them.

'You're Miss Fry's Goddaughter.' And he had smiled, at once, at her startled look. 'Oh, don't you know how it is? Everyone knows everything here. And tells.'

Oh.' She would have said, 'I don't know you,' but could not.

'Have you come to live here?'

'Only — I don't know. For a while. Perhaps until the autumn. I don't know.'

'Miss Fry is a good, true person.' It should have sounded strange – from anyone else it would have sounded strange, but this was Ben's way, she was used to it from the beginning. And it was right, her Godmother was so, a 'good, true person'.

Ben said what he thought or felt, and expected it to be accepted, there was no duplicity in him, and because she had no experience of how men behaved towards women, of the possible devices of human evasion, of flattery and pretence, she believed him, when he said, 'I hope you stay here.' Though often, later, Ben's directness was to startle her, cause her to draw back and consider. Other people were no longer startled, they accepted from Ben things which no one else would say to them.

Suddenly, she had felt no anxiety in talking to him, it was the easiest thing, she told him about her father and Ellen, about home, and how she liked it here, what she did every day, where she had been, and he listened, sitting very still, not fidgeting with anything. Remembering that, she thought, he sat still that first time, and on the night before he died, he was eased of his usual restless need to be up and working, occupying his hands. And the two occasions formed the beginning and the end of a complete circle, a small circle, but one within which she seemed to have spent the whole of her life. He had got up, to go on with his work, and she had walked away, up the slope between the beeches, thinking of what he had said, how he looked, and only when she came out into the sunlit lane did she stop, realising that he had not asked her name, though she knew his. She wished that she might go back and tell him.

*

The days lengthened, moving towards midsummer, spun out like fine, golden threads, and Godmother Fry watched her, seeing the change, though she said nothing. Until the Sunday, when he came to the house, and by then, he knew her name, and wanted to take her to Cantlow Hill, with a picnic. Then, everything had fallen into place, and she was not surprised at it, only felt more than ever in possession of herself and of the world.

Cantlow Hill. It was six miles away but she was good at walking.

'There,' he had said, and pointed to the small stone church at the top, surrounded by sweet-chestnut trees, which spread out long fingers of shade. They went up the close-turfed hill, between sheep, which cantered away at the sight of them, bleating anxious calls to one another, and the calls echoed and were taken up all around them. The air was dry and fragrant with hay-dust, and just ahead, it danced and shimmered with the reflected heat.

She saw Ben every day for the next three weeks,

but it was that first time, at Cantlow Hill, which she brought back to mind over and over again.

She had kept glancing at him and each time, she expected him to have vanished. When she looked away again, down the hill to where the fields and woods and the flat beige ribbon of road lay, and Cantlow village, rose-red under the sun, everything seemed to have changed, everything was somehow caught up in her happiness. She loved everything she saw, for itself and because it existed in the same world as Ben.

He took her inside the church, where it was as cool as a dairy, and there was a curious, sandy light. It was a very plain church. He showed her the carvings of animals and birds that ran round the tops of all the stone pillars, and the wall paintings of the Virgin and Child, just showing flaky blue and cream, by the altar. The pews were of pale wood, and there were no coloured windows, no embroidered hangings or kneelers, and so the shapes of the archways and pillars and roof were clear. And the outside world was set in the frame of the porch, like a picture, vividly green and blazing with sunlight, the band of the sky vibrating faintly at the edge. From far away, they heard the sheep cries and from the churchyard, blackbirds and the churr of wood pigeons.

They ate their picnic, eggs and apples and cheese and bread, sitting on the cool grass among the gravestones, and Ruth had closed her eyes and prayed for this never to end.

*

The scents of the day hung about in the warm evening air, the sky seemed not to darken but to grow paler and paler, losing its colour, and the trees and hedges threw blackberry shadows, and every sound was separately held, like the air within a soap bubble.

They went down through the woods to a stream and picked handfuls of dark watercress, and crushed wild thyme under their feet. The water was as clear as glass and very shallow, running over silvery pebbles. Ruth lay down and put her hands in it up to the wrists, and they took on a strange phosphorescence as the water slipped between her fingers. She touched the thin, cold stalks of weed.

The light became mossy-green, and a slight, warm breeze stirred the tops of the trees, with a sound like the very distant sea.

'Well,' Godmother Fry had said, when she got in, 'well!' and had held out her hand, and brought Ruth closer to her chair, looked into her face, knowing.

8

Ruth saw the man first from the window. She had been up for half an hour, perhaps more, had washed and dressed; and then done nothing but stand here, looking out, too tired to think or feel, drugged with the night's heavy sleep.

It had stopped raining but the sky above the sagging trees was dough-coloured. She had not wanted to wake, for what could she do with another day, how might she drag herself through eight or ten hours, struggling against remembering too much and falling into despair, or giving in and weeping uselessly, sickening herself. She had taken to going to bed earlier, at seven or eight o'clock, longing for the oblivion which always came to her.

The man was old and dirty and pushed a handcart with one lop-sided wheel. He came over the track, looking down, but making directly towards the cottage and at first she thought that someone was again trying to see her, to pry, under the pretence of bringing her this or that, and she shrank back from the window.

But he was not from the village, she had never seen

him before. As he came nearer, she noticed that the cart was half-full, though she could not tell with what, and loosely covered with a tattered sheet of sacking or canvas. Then he was one of the travelling men, selling pots and pans and brushes. She wanted nothing, she would have opened the window and called to him to go away. But she did not, it seemed impossible for her to exert herself even as much as that. And so he came on, leaving the hand cart at the gate and trudging down the path and around to the back door. Well, he would go away, as they all did, she had only to wait.

But after his second or third knocking, she went down, suddenly wanting to have the sight, even for a moment, of another human face, to be in touch again with the real world, outside of herself. Jo had not come yet today.

He was not old, not really, only dirty, with a thin face and stiff limbs. She thought, he does not know me or anything about me, he does not know about Ben. But he must, everyone must know – how could there be a person in the world who did not?

He had begun to speak as she opened the door, a stream of words, pattered off like a rhyme, spoken dozens of times each day.

'Old clothes, shoes, pots, pans, vases, plates, watches or clocks, working or not, silver, coins, medals, knives, scissors, ornaments, fire-irons, coal-scuttles, blankets, brass …'

'All that?'

'Any of that, any ...'

'How? On that cart? How can you have all of that to sell?'

He pulled off his cap and set it back on his head in a single movement, but there was time for her to see that the hair was growing only here and there, in tufts and patches, anyhow, and with scaly, bald places between, like the pelt of an animal with mange.

'To sell, young lady, anything to sell, old clothes, shoes, pots, pans...'

'No,' she said at once, for of course there was nothing and even if there had been, what would she be doing selling it to a travelling man?

He did not stop until he reached the end of his chant again, like a clock which had been wound up and must run right down, could not be interrupted.

Ruth looked past him, at the garden, the soil clogged after days of rain, the path sticky and red with clay. The donkey Balaam stood by the fence, head hanging down as though on a broken neck, stood as she had been standing at her window, scarcely alive.

'I've nothing.'

'Good money for your old things.'

'There's nothing.'

He turned away, thinking, that he'd not waste any more time here, on a young woman who looked as if she were not long married, and just setting up home, having little. It was the old who had always something to sell, the old and the very poor.

It came to her in a flash, then, she knew what she should do, wanted to do, for maybe it would help her, maybe this way she could forget, could somehow try to begin her life afresh. She knew.

'Wait!'

He stopped, glanced back over his shoulder.

'If ... if you come back... come back later.'

'Afternoon?'

'Yes. Yes, come then. Then I'll have things – a lot of things. I want to sell ...'

He did not reply, and she called out again, as he reached the top gate, 'You will? Please come back, please...'

He touched his cap, nodded and took up the cart. A thin drizzle had begun to fall again.

The idea had taken hold of her like some kind of madness, she was possessed only by the passionate need for it to be accomplished, and there seemed to be so little time. Ah, but when it was over, when she had done it, all of it and the man had been again and gone, then, then...

But she must think. Now. She would begin upstairs.

At first, she pulled out drawers and cupboards at random, half-emptied them, flung things down on the floor or the bed, swept whole shelves bare. Then she realised that there had to be some order to it or she would never be through, and went out into the shed, found some old grain sacks which were slightly damp and smelled of mice, but were still strong enough, they would serve. Into these she shovelled the things, coats, shirts, shoes, trousers, jumpers, one after another, anyhow, and when the clothes were done, she went downstairs, for there was so much, he had had so many things, she had never realised. There were tools, books, pipes, keys, things in the bureau, and all of them went into the sacks, and she would not let herself examine anything closely or stop to think, she hardly let her hands touch them. She kept only one or two things; the rose-quartz, and the magnifying glass, and a leather belt with a silver buckle, and his pocket watch, which she would give to Jo. There was a seal ring, which Ben had never worn, but it had belonged to his grandfather, he had liked to pick it up and look at it sometimes. She would keep that one thing for herself. But nothing else, nothing.

The bedroom looked quite different, it belonged clearly now to one person only. Except for the bed. And seeing it, she wanted that to be gone, too, and perhaps the man with the handcart had some friend who would come for it, or else there might be someone else she could give it to. It was an old, brass bed, high and wide, and had belonged, like so much of the furniture in the cottage, to Godmother Fry. But in the small room was a small bed, and she wanted that in here, and would have exchanged them at once if she had been able to move them on her own; so strong was her desire to change things utterly, to have nothing of Ben and the old life left here, no reminders. She liked to think of sleeping in a very narrow bed, bound about tightly with sheets, so that there could be no space of mattress and pillow to which she might, out of longing or habit, turn in the night.

The door of the large wardrobe hung open. She stared into the depths of it, put her hand inside and felt only space and the length of smooth round rail, where his clothes had hung.

The sacks were heavy, she had to drag them, bumping behind her, down the stairs, and she put them in the kitchen close to the door, and then waited for the afternoon to come, and the man with the handcart, she could do or think of nothing else, could not move forward in time until everything had gone.

She did not worry at all about what any of them might say, the family, other people in the village, or even of what Ben would have thought. She could only feel for herself, and the things were hers now, weren't they, she might do as she chose with them and what use were they to her? It was this, or else give his clothes away to men in the village, and then see them wearing what had belonged to him, had covered his flesh, and that she could not have borne.

As the morning went on, the drizzle condensed into a mist which rolled up the garden and across the common, closing in upon the cottage, until she could neither hear nor see anything outside and so, none of it concerned her, she was estranged from all people, all life, and wanted it that way. Perhaps they did, too.

They did not wish to see her, because they were embarrassed or hostile, and she reminded them of too much, brought death too close to them. They thought, but shied away, at once, from those thoughts.

It was almost five o'clock and her heart had begun to thump hard with the fear that he might not come back, she walked in and out of the rooms, and stood, first at the front window, then at the back, she prayed for him to come, for if he did not, how could she live with those sacks, piled up by the door, like bodies awaiting burial. She would not be able to open them and take everything out, restore the things to their old places, she could not bear to think of touching them again. She remembered the children in the wood. Well, she would copy them; somehow, she would drag the sacks down to the meadow, or into the copse, and either bury them or make a pyre and burn them in the garden.

But he came back, when the mist was thickening and darkening, she heard the rattle of the loose wheel over the path. The handcart was empty now.

He leaned over one of the sacks, pulled apart the string she had tied roughly round the top, and was going to tip the things out on to the kitchen floor.

'No!'

She grabbed at his arm in her panic, for she must not see any of them ever again.

'Take them. I just want you to take them away.'

'I have to see what's there, don't I, what's any good?'

'No ... it's ... I don't want you to open them.'

He stood upright slowly, and stared at her.

'There are clothes. . . men's . . . everything, and tools and... it's all good.'

'You say...'

'I don't care what you give me for them – anything, please, take them all away, please.'

For you will hear, she thought, they will tell you, any of them, pass the story down through the village, say where you've been, who gave you these things, and they will tell you all you want to know.

He said nothing else. He lifted the sacks on to the handcart, covered them over with the canvas sheet, gave her some money, and Ruth did not look at it, or at him, again, she closed the door and went back, hid in the corner of the room, so that she need not see the loaded cart, though she heard it, and his footsteps, going away through the fog.

She was trembling with relief, and tiredness, and with shame too, for she was afraid of what she had done, and angry, and startled by how violently the need to get rid of everything had taken her, how urgently she had acted.

The room was dark. After a long time, she opened her hand which was holding the money, and looked down. A few coins. She did not count them. They felt dirty, she seemed to be holding thirty pieces of silver, the betrayal was so great. And just as she had needed to empty the house of Ben's possessions, so, now, the one thing she must do was to get rid of this evil money

She ran out of the house and down the garden through the soaking mist, struggled over the fence into the meadow and went on, running, running, stumbling on tussocks of grass and soaking her feet and ankles with wet and mud, she was gasping, her chest burned She had to push her way through the undergrowth, briars and black, tangled roots and branches, tearing her clothes, to get into the copse, and here, the mud was thicker, she fell once and gashed her hand on something, and struggled up again, bleeding and coated with a mulch of sodden leaves. She could not see, only grope her way to the top of the slope, beyond which the coppice dropped down steeply towards the beech woods. It was there, into the black space that fell away at her feet, that she flung the money, and turned away at once, not wanting to hear it fall, began to run again, back through the mud and bushes and sodden grass of the meadow, to the cottage, and there, surely, she would feel clean, for she had thrown everything far away from her, she had not even counted the money, she had done her penance.

But she had not. She knew, as she opened the door into that house, from which she had so violently banished everything of Ben. She stood, looking down at herself, at the torn, soiled clothes and shoes, at the caked mud and the smears of blood on her hand and arm.

And dropped to her knees then, and wept for forgiveness.

9

The days had been grey forever, there had always been rain and mist, and Lent would not come to an end.

But when she awoke, in the very early morning of the day after the travelling man had been, the sun was rising and spreading out through the room. When she went to the window, she looked out upon a gold and green world, upon spring. It was the end of April, it was Easter Saturday; and she understood that the forgiveness had come.

It no longer mattered about the empty drawers and cupboards, she closed them, and dressed and went through the house, opening every window wide, though the air which came in was still quite cold. But she wanted that, fresh air and light, everything must be light.

In the larder, she found a small loaf of bread, wrapped in white cloth, which Jo must have left for her, and though it was no longer very moist, she cut and buttered and ate it, slice after slice, before going down to let out the hens and bring up the eggs.

And the eggs themselves looked different, no

longer, dull, heavy things, pale as stones; she cracked open two and beat them up with butter and they were golden yellow, glistening and sweet in the pan. She felt as if she had never eaten food before. It was a new gift, everything was a gift, and what she knew, above all else, was that she must take it, take it and be glad, not only for her own sake but for Ben's. This was what he had been waiting for, and wanting. It might not last.

By eight o'clock Jo was here, and as she saw him coming towards her through the sunlight, he, too, looked changed, his hair and pale skin were like those of a new-born child, he walked with a grace and lightness Ruth had never seen before. He stopped, and saw her face, and smiled, all anxiety gone from him.

He said, 'Tomorrow...'

'Easter. Yes. Oh, and I'd forgotten, Jo – how could I have forgotten?'

For Easter had been so important. Fleetingly, she remembered last year, when it had been much earlier, in March, and still really winter.

'We should go,' Jo said, 'or I'll go, if you don't want to. I shall understand – if you'd rather not. But somebody must go.'

He looked about him, and up at the sky, over the copse, 'It's the best sort of day. You don't always get a day like this for it.'

He was talking about gathering the flowers, in the woods and along banks and hedgerows, and moss from beside the stream. On Easter Saturday evening, people took them up to the churchyard and spent hours, dressing the graves, making beautiful floral patterns on the turf, they worked until it was dark and even later, by lantern light, so that, on the following morning, all the dead should be decked out with fresh-growing blooms, a resurrection.

'I shan't mind, if you want me to go and do it on my own.'

'Oh, no. No.'

Because this was the first real thing she could do for Ben, and she wanted to have the pleasure of it, of going with Jo about the countryside, filling up the baskets with damp green moss and spring flowers.

'No, we must go together.'

Jo frowned, and glanced away from her.

'And the others?' Ruth said.

He shrugged.

'Well – Alice might come.'

But he shook his head.

All the colours of that day were green and gold, even the sky seemed to have taken on a reflection from the white-gold sun and the upturned petals of yellow flowers in field and meadow, and along the margins of the woods.

As they stood at the top of the field for a moment, looking down, Ruth and Jo saw, first, the haze of green, like an openwork shawl laid over the tops of all the trees, where the buds were unfolding into first leaf. Ruth thought that she could never have seen so many different shades of green; the emerald of the larches that fringed the beech woods, and the yellowish-green early poplars, ash green willow leaves and the pale, oaten-olive tinge of the young wheat. The grass was green, dark as moss in the shadow of the banks, and clear as lime, high up in the full sun, and when they went into the wood, the light was pond-green and, at their feet, the polished green blades of bluebells.

They went right down through the beeches, which sloped to the stream, and passed by the exact place where Ruth had first spoken to Ben, and she knew it, and did not stop, did not mind, she felt only contentment.

This was the same stream, flowing quite quickly today, into which she and Ben had looked down at their own faces, which had shimmered and changed, as the water rippled. Jo began to pull up the soft sphagnum moss and line the flat, open baskets with it. It was curled close and springy as a child's head of hair, and sweet, damp-smelling. They were careful to take enough of the soil clinging to it, so that the moss would not wither before the day was out, and would lie well on top of the graves. They worked quietly, happily, moving up the bank, trying not to slip; but once, Ruth did stumble over, so that her foot went into the water; it was stinging cold. But it did not matter, nothing could be wrong. Here and there, the wood was darker, but the beech leaves were still light, they would not be out until the first week in May, and so, almost everywhere, the sun shone through, their hands and faces were gilded and the stones under the water of the stream shone in flat, translucent ovals or glinted up in points of light. They were ready to pick the flowers.

'Yellow,' Jo said, laughing, 'it's all yellow – it's like finding – treasure, coins, under the sea.

There were lemon primroses, and the deeper tinted cowslips, celandines and rich marsh-marigolds, the last of the miniature daffodils, and dandelions, bright as medallions – which might be weeds but were beautiful enough for any grave.

Hidden in among all this gold were the white and mauve flowers, ladies' smocks and dark wood violets and anemones, periwinkle, and then the sorrel with shell-pink streaks. They went home, to water the baskets and put them on the cool slab of the larder, before setting out again, this time to gather so many bluebells that they could not help but drop some, and so, they left a trail of misty blue all the way up the fields and the lane. Ruth's hands were stained and slimy with the sap that oozed out of the glutinous stems, she put her face down into the flowers and smelled the smell of spring, and felt dizzy with it. Then, she looked at Jo as he walked beside her, his skin ruddy at the end of the day's sunshine, and for the first time, she saw in him some resemblance to Ben, some fleeting expression of eyes and mouth. It did not give her any sense of shock, it comforted her, and she loved Jo more – because of this, but because he was also so much himself, was linked by blood to his dead brother and yet was such a different person.

*

As they walked up the slope towards the church, she saw that others were already there, figures bent over, or kneeling around the graves, working, and for a second, she wanted to turn back and run from them, for they might stare, or even speak to her, and she would know what they were thinking, about herself and about Ben, they would intrude.

It was seven o'clock, there would be an hour more of the evening light, which was paler now, as though the sun had faded in colour as it had lost its warmth. The old headstones threw blurred shadows across the grass.

As they went through the gate, Jo moved a little nearer to her, protective, knowing what she felt, and perhaps he needed help from her, too. Those people who turned, hearing the new footsteps, turned back at once, lowered their heads. No one stared. So it was the same. They did not trust her, they were suspicious and nervous of her, after the stories they had been hearing these past weeks. Perhaps already the story of yesterday and her sale of Ben's things to the travelling man, had reached them. Ruth held up her head.

But it was not to Ben's grave that they went first. Godmother Fry was buried at the front of the church, under a plain buff headstone, and it was for her that Ruth had brought the blue and white and pale mauve flowers, which had been her favourites; her own garden had always been thick with snowdrops in January and forget-me-nots in April and May, in the shade of the lavender bushes.

Jo spread the moss, pressing it firmly into the ground, and Ruth picked out the shape of a cross with the flowers, mixing them together anyhow, for that was how her Godmother had liked them, not separated or planted out in orderly rows.

They had only half-finished, when she heard a step directly behind her, a shadow lay over the moss. She looked up.

'Ruth – I'd not expected you – not this year. I'd come to do it for you.'

Miss Clara – Godmother Fry's neighbour and friend for over thirty years, Miss Clara, small and shrunken, with crippled bones, her hands and feet swollen and hardened with rheumatism. But she had come, with a basketful of blue flowers, she had been going to kneel and dress the grave, no matter that her limbs would be so stiff she might hardly be able to hobble home afterwards.

'I'd have been glad to do it. You ...'

Jo glanced anxiously at Ruth. But she did not mind, she would say it.

'We're going to Ben's grave next, with the yellow flowers.'

Miss Clara. Ruth had forgotten her; if she had been at Ben's funeral, she had not noticed. And she was not a person who would ever have intruded or pried or gossiped. She realised that since the death of Godmother Fry, Miss Clara must have been lonely, and she felt a dart of grief and pity, and of guilt, too, for she might have done something, might have visited her and talked. But she had been too wrapped up, first within the warm womb of her happiness with Ben, and then in the cold shell of grief. She had not thought of anyone.

She said, 'You'd like to help – you'd like us to use your flowers.'

For Miss Clara was standing, looking down anxiously at what they had already done, not wanting to go away again.

'Jo...'

He stood up at once, and took Miss Clara's basket.

'It's very cold,' Ruth said, 'and damp, too – you shouldn't kneel. But if you tell Jo – if you show him how you'd like it to be...'

She saw the gratitude in Miss Clara's eyes.

Jo said, 'I'll come over to you, Ruth – when I've finished it. Wait for me to come.'

'Of course.'

And then she went alone, around the side of the church, carrying her basket of moss and golden flowers, she began alone, to dress Ben's grave. It was darker here, the sun had dropped down behind the tower.

The moss felt like seaweed, and the turf of the new-mounded grave was cold. She thought, then, of that other body, carried away from the terrible cross at dusk, and the great stone rolled in front of the tomb, imagined how it must have been inside, echoing and fusty as a cave, with the limp figure drained of all its blood and bound about in cloths, she felt, within herself, the bewilderment and fear and despair of those men and women.

'Ben,' she said once, and rested her hand on a part of the turf she had not yet dressed with moss. But she felt only calmness, still, and did not try to imagine whatever might be underneath the soil now.

She could scarcely see the colour of the flowers, they were no longer bright, as they had been when she picked them, and would be again, tomorrow, under the first sun. The cross she made was dense, each flower packed tightly to the next one, so that the spiked petals of the dandelions and the rounded buttercups overlapped, with the primroses pushed between.

By the time Jo came over to her, it was almost dark and the grave was nearly finished. Ruth's back and legs ached.

She handed the basket to Jo.

'You should do some – part of it ought to be yours.'

She stood up and rubbed her hands over her neck and shoulders. The air smelled of the moist flowers.

'Miss Clara went home. She said to tell you . . .' he hesitated.

"What?'

'To tell you – she said, "I've had her in my mind. I've thought about her, every day."

Some of the other people had brought lanterns and the churchyard was lit here and there by their unsteady, silvery light, rings of it lay about the grass and the graves like glow-worms. Ruth caught the quick sight of some face, turned momentarily towards the lamp. But there were no sounds. Jo said, pausing for a moment, and resting back on his heels, 'Tomorrow ...' and there was an excitement in his voice, 'Tomorrow, think how it will be!'

Yes, Ruth thought, and so it will be, for it is true, and the sun will shine and the grave-flowers will be like the raiment of the risen dead. But if he is risen, where do I find him, or see him? How can I know?

She was tired enough, in her body and her mind, to lie down, here and now, and sleep, as these men and women were sleeping, and wait for the new life of the morning.

'Jo...'

'Yes, we'll go now. It's finished, isn't it?'

'It's finished.'

The baskets were empty, light as air, Jo swung them both from his hands. The people who were left had gathered together in groups, not far from the path, murmuring to one another, shifting their lanterns, but as Ruth and Jo passed they fell silent and did not move, perhaps they would none of them ever look at her, or speak again? Well, she would bear it, and they were not the ones to blame.

Someone was standing in the middle of the path, just beyond the gate. Jo stopped dead. But Ruth went on, close enough to see his face, and as she looked up into it, it came over her again, as when she had seen Miss Clara, this intense awareness of another person's suffering, and shame at the way she had excluded all thought of it.

Arthur Bryce looked old; the injured arm and shoulder drooped and Ruth saw that he did not know how to speak to her, dared not begin.

Now, Jo was beside her. 'I was coming,' he said defensively, 'I'd have been home soon.'

'No ...' His father shook his head and shifted his feet on the gravel. 'I'd have known you were here. I'd not have worried.'

No, for none of them ever did, Jo had always told her that. 'They don't notice me, they don't care what I do.'

Was that true? How could she know what Arthur Bryce truly felt about the death of his elder son and about the younger one, who kept himself outside their circle? He was not a man who would ever reveal his thoughts or emotions, because of awkwardness and also because he himself did not fully understand them. Ruth thought I have never been close to him, never tried to reach him, he is the father of Ben, without him, Ben would never have existed, and yet he might be a stranger. They seemed to have come face to face for the first time in their lives.

She said, 'Will you go and look at the grave?'

'I thought... I just wanted to come.' But he did not move.

'We've dressed it, it's beautiful ... it's a golden cross. All the flowers are gold,' Jo said, 'but you wouldn't be able to see it now. You ought to wait until morning.'

Someone passed them, carrying a lamp.

'It was only right someone should come.'

'Alice ...'

'No. She goes out – somewhere. She's always out, these nights.'

And Ruth knew, without needing to ask, that Dora Bryce would be beside the fire, keening, and would complain to them all when they got home, would say, 'Did you expect me to go? Up there in the dark on my hands and knees? Did you expect me to be able to bear that, and my own son only just in his grave? And what does any of it mean – Easter, when he was taken from me?'

But I have been the same, she said, I have locked myself up and been selfish and bitter and full of doubts and my own pity, where is the difference between us, in all truth?

'I'll get back. I'd only wanted to see if it was done.'

Jo burst out angrily, 'Did you think it wouldn't be? That we'd forget? How could you think Ruth wouldn't be here, and me? We...'

Ruth laid a hand on his arm.

'Walk with us,' she said to Arthur Bryce. And at last, something was between them, she recognised it in his face, uncertain affection and grief for her, a desire to say and do what was right, what would please her. He wanted to walk with them and not to be, or to feel, alone. He wanted her love. And knew that he had it, as she went along between him and Jo, down towards the village. None of them spoke, but they were bound together and the past was redeemed.

At the bottom of the lane, he said, 'You don't want to go up there, over that common, you oughtn't to be on your own.'

'It isn't late.'

'It's dark.'

'I'm used to it. I'm not afraid of the dark.'

Jo said at once, 'But I'll go with you, I always do. I'll take you.'

'No. Go home, Jo. Go with your father.'

For someone else needed the boy's company and strength, she had clung on to him too selfishly all these weeks past, and it would not be losing him, to send him now, with Arthur Bryce, back to his mother, his own home, not losing but sharing.

Ruth set off down the slope, carrying the baskets, full of a quiet joy.

*

She could not imagine why she had ever thought of moving the bed; it was familiar and she felt secure in it, cradled by the soft mounds of the feather mattress which were impressed with her own shape.

And tomorrow was Easter Day.

Then, as she lay there, she recalled, vividly, the conversation she and Ben had had last year, on Good Friday. They had been walking through the beech woods, but it was too cold, her hands and face had felt flayed and sore, and her head ached in the east wind, they came home. The weather had seemed to underline the day's significance. Between twelve o'clock and three, the sky had blackened and a sudden blizzard had swirled up the garden, the gale battered at the cottage windows.

'Listen to it!'

Ben had looked up from his book. 'They used to say the birds all stopped singing, for those three hours. That everything went quiet, except for the wind.'

'They used to say that the cattle knelt down in their stalls at midnight on Christmas Eve.'

'You could still find those who believe it.'

'Do you?'

'It's only a way of putting things.' He got up and walked to the window to watch the storm.

'And will the sun shine again, at three o'clock?'

'Oh, sooner than that today. Look.'

He pointed up to the clouds, already parting in the wind, like rags being shredded by rough pairs of hands, revealing smears of blue. Hail lay on the grass but it would soon melt.

Ruth went to stand beside him. Then he said, 'One day...'

'One day what?'

Ben hesitated. 'I often think about it. About dying. Times like this. Today.'

'No!'

He looked at her in surprise.

'Don't you?'

'I – I don't know. But I don't like Good Friday, I want it to be over.'

'Why?'

'I want it to be Easter Day.'

'But you must have Good Friday first.'

'I'm going to make the dinner now.'

'Ruth? Don't you think about dying?'

'No. I don't know.'

Though it was not long since Godmother Fry's peaceful death, and she had thought about it then, and it had seemed a good thing, natural and right, Godmother Fry had been very old, and waiting for death, happy to receive it.

Ruth shook her head. 'Not yet. Not for me or for you.'

'Of course – for me and for you.'

'No – when we're old, and if we are very ill. Then. And I think about it when animals die. But that's all different.'

'Why? And why should you mind it? If you think about dying, you know that it ...'

'I don't want to think about it.'

'But it doesn't matter. In the end, dying doesn't matter. Can't you see?'

'It doesn't mean we have to think about it and talk about it. Not now. Not yet.'

'Yes.'

She had heard and remembered but never truly understood what he said that day.

'It does mean that. It is all around us and within us and outside of us. Us. And once you know that, then it doesn't matter at all.'

She had clutched hold of his arm, then, in sudden dread, and to try and bring him back to her, to this world here and now, she was afraid of his distance from her when he spoke like this, afraid of the things he seemed to know, and of what might happen.

'Don't... don't talk about it, you mustn't talk about dying. You must never, never die. I won't let you die.'

'Ah, Ruth.' And he had looked at her, his face full of a kind of sadness, and knowledge, 'Ah, Ruth.'

It was as though he had just spoken to her, now, aloud in this quiet bedroom, she could see every detail of his face. And he had had to die.

She sat up, startled. Where had that come from? How did she think of that? For it was not a phrase remembered, nor a fancy. It was a piece of truth, and vital to her. *He had had to die.*

She lay back on the pillows, unable to comprehend it. But quite certain. She slept, and dreamed no dreams, and woke, at the sound of the first bird call, in the pearly dawn of Easter Day.

*

Yesterday, the world had been full of flowers and trees; today, it was the birds that she saw everywhere, as she walked to church in the early morning. The sun shone again, as Jo had said it would, though the grass was heavy with dew, her shoes were soaked before she reached the top of the garden. Low down in the bushes, chiff-chaffs pinked out their sharp, repeated notes, and high up, spiralling until they were almost out of sight, were the larks, streaming with song. In the fields she saw pheasants, the clever and the lucky ones who had escaped the gun, and were free now, the shooting season over; the trailing tails of the cocks glowed gold and copper and rust red. Everything was singing, it was as though she could hear the faint, high humming as the world turned. She thought, I am still happy, I am still sane; and was certain that it would last, at least for today and perhaps for as long as the sun shone. She seemed to be lifted a little way out of herself, to be floating above the ground.

Jo was waiting for her at the corner of the lane, looking serious and suddenly older, taller, in his dark

Sunday suit. Today, she could see in him no resemblance to Ben at all.

The last time she had been inside the church was for Ben's funeral. Well, she would not brood about that, it was over and she must think only about this day, trying to understand. And she must go in among all the people and never mind if they stared at her and judged her. But seeing them walking up the hill ahead, and a group standing in the church porch, she clenched her hands tightly, and it seemed that her heart would leap up into her mouth.

'Oh, Ruth, look! Look.'

They had reached the lych-gate. Jo was pointing. She looked.

Had she been blind last year? Had it looked like this? The churchyard was brilliant as a garden with the patterned flowers, almost every grave was decked out in growing white and blue, pink and butter-yellow, and underneath it all, the watery moss and the vivid grass; it was as though all the people had indeed truly risen and were dancing in the sunshine, there was nothing but rejoicing and release. She walked slowly across the turf to the side of the church and stood, looking towards Ben's grave. It was like a sunburst. She did not need, or want, to go nearer.

Jo touched her arm. 'You see,' he said, his voice full of wonder, 'it did happen. It does. It's true.'

'Did you ever doubt it?'

'Once,' he said carefully, 'one time.'

Only once. Ruth realised how close to Ben he was, in his way of seeing and understanding the world; he had the same clear grasp of the truth that lay beneath the surface of things, he saw, as she had only glimpsed once or twice, the whole pattern. They had the gift of angels.

Stepping into the church was like stepping into some sunlit clearing of the woods; there were flowers and leaves and the scents of them everywhere, the altar and pulpit, the font and the rails were wound about with ropes of white and golden blossoms, the ledges were banked with bluebells on mounds of moss, and the sun shone in through the windows, sending rippling coloured lights on to the stone walls, catching fire on the brass of the cross and the lectern. Ruth felt nothing but happiness, she walked down between the high wooden pews right to the front of the church, and looked here and there and smiled, if she caught someone's eye, and did not mind that they seemed embarrassed, uncertain of her. She went into the same pew and for a second saw again how it had been that other day, with the long pale coffin that had seemed to fill the whole building, the whole world.

But what she became aware of after that was not the presence of the village people sitting or kneeling behind her, but of others, the church was full of all those who had ever prayed in it, the air was crammed and vibrating with their goodness and the freedom and power of their resurrection, and she felt herself to be part of some great, living and growing tapestry, every thread of which joined with and crossed and belonged to every other, though each one was also entirely and distinctly itself. She heard again the strange music in her head and her ears, and yet somewhere far outside of them.

But it also came to her that she might, after all, be simply going out of her mind, and she wondered if grief could become a sort of madness, which did not only cause one to weep and to despair, but to be light-headed, with invisible sights and unheard sounds, imaginary consolations.

She opened her eyes again and saw the flowers and the sun on the walls, and these were real, living and beautiful, she was not imagining them or the joy they gave her, the reassurance; and when the clergy came in and they stood to sing the Easter hymn, she felt for the first time, not since Ben's death, but since coming here at all, that she truly belonged, that these people were part of her life, as she was of theirs, and there was no need for her suspicion and hostility, her pride and fear, these were dangerous, cancerous, and could, in the end, destroy her. Everything, everything, she saw and believed and understood, that Easter morning. She knelt. She said, 'I shall never do wrong again. I shall not weep out of pity for myself, or doubt what is true or fail to be grateful. I shall be well. I shall be well.' And it seemed impossible that it should not be so, she was so full of strength and purpose and assurance, so far away from the nights of bitterness and despair.

Nothing could ever harm her again.

Coming out of the church, so elated and charged with resolution, she found herself separated from Jo, and beside some of the others, those she had smiled at going in to the service; and now she wanted to speak to them, too, to show them how much she had changed, and that she no longer dreaded the sight of them, no longer wanted to cut herself off. But the words would not come, she was shy, and so, waited for one of them to approach her and begin, to make it easier for her; she looked expectantly from face to face.

And she saw that they had not changed, that they still feared her, and the taint of death and grief she carried upon herself, still smarted from the rebuffs she had so violently dealt to their offers of help and sympathy, still resented her pride. They had learned to keep their distance, because that was what she had wanted; why should they recognise any change now?

She saw them turn away, after swift, uneasy glances at her, watched as they went off, in twos and threes down the church path, and felt the full force of their rejection. She wanted to shout after them, make them understand, that it was Easter and a new life, that she wanted to be different, and where was their charity, why were they not ready to take her among them, by saying a few words, to welcome her? How could they ever expect her to make this new start entirely alone?

But she knew, she knew. She was reaping what she had sown. She felt faint with a sudden, overwhelming desire to have Ben with her, shielding her from the rest of this hostile world, for then, she would never want anyone or anything else, they could all go their way.

She looked about her. Everything was the same. Everything had changed. The world was quite empty, although the sun still shone, the birds sang, darting about the flowered churchyard, just as only moments ago and ever since yesterday morning, it had been brimming full; there seemed nothing whatsoever that might comfort her or give her strength and protection. When Jo came out of the church at last, she saw him for what he was, a young boy, vulnerable and with his own needs, his own life to live, not someone she could ultimately depend upon.

But what had happened? And why, why? After she had prayed and been so certain, so confident of herself, after the words of the resurrection had sounded in her ears and meant that she had all power, all possessions? She felt deceived, tricked. The people had excluded her, had not let her make any fresh beginning. Well then, she would do without them still.

'Jo – listen, if you go home and change out of your suit, I'll make a picnic, it will be hot all day – we can go right over the ridge, we can walk all the way to the river if you like, we...'

Jo looked at her miserably.

'Ruth – Ruth, I can't. I can't go with you anywhere.'

'Can't?'

'I want to – I'd rather be with you, only ... I have to go and see Grandmother Holmes at Dutton Reach, we're all going, I promised I would when I was walking back home last night – I told my father. I have to go now.'

Yes, of course he had to go. She could not always have Jo, he did not belong to her. However much she might dislike them, his family had some claim upon him, it was right that he should visit his grandmother.

'Of course – I didn't realise. Of course you must go.'

'But you ...'

'Oh Jo, don't look like that, don't worry. I can do lots of things. The garden – I ought to do something in the garden, and go and see Miss Clara, too – she might not be well, she wasn't in the church.'

'I don't want you to be by yourself.'

'I'm all right, Jo. I shall be all right.'

'It's just that I do have to go, I promised.'

'Yes. It's Easter. Your grandmother will want to see you – all of you.'

'I'll come up tomorrow, I won't leave you for another whole day.'

'Jo...'

'Yes?'

She wanted to tell him that he was good and she loved him, that he must never let her take advantage of him, never forsake his own freedom, his own life. But she said nothing, in the end, only put a hand on his shoulder as they walked away from the church.

*

She knew that the fault was not in the world but in herself and so, it was her own self that she hated and wanted to be free of, as she sat outside in the afternoon sun. But she was the same, just as her situation, her widowhood was the same and would not alter. Yesterday had been a delusion, too full of hope and contentment, too soon; yesterday, gathering the flowers and dressing the grave, she thought she had accepted completely that she was alone now, and would not see Ben again on this earth, and could bear it, had enough strength and to spare.

She could not bear it or believe it. And if this was all there ever would be, if she was to be lifted up and then hurled down again upon her face, and never certain of anything, then she could not go on living at all, for neither joy nor mourning, pleasure or pain seemed to have any final meaning.

In the middle of that morning, she had gone down to the village, to Miss Clara's house, wanting company, now that Jo was away with the Bryces to Dutton Reach. She did not resent that, only missed him, and envied this new closeness in the family from which she had always deliberately excluded herself.

Miss Clara was out, the house was locked up, front and back. So she had friends, after all, or relatives, people Ruth knew nothing about.

And now, the house was empty of him and what lay under the flowered grave diminished with every hour and would soon be nothing. She doubted that Ben had ever existed.

She closed her eyes but that gave her no relief from the turmoil inside her head; rather, it grew worse, it was like dark blood, boiling up and spilling over, confusing her utterly; she saw it behind her eyelids and was giddy, she had to look out again at something, anything, a tree or the donkey or the stone beside her left hand, to steady herself. In the end, she wept with exhaustion, lying on the grass, and rubbing her hands to and fro. 'Oh God, Oh God... I knew ... I don't, I don't know anything... Oh God, I am mad.'

She was shocked at the sound of the words, spoken aloud. 'I am mad.' She lay still and the earth teemed beneath her. 'I am mad.' And she waited for some final, appalling explosion, waited for the light to spin and fall inwards upon her, breaking and smashing open like a wave, to find that she was indeed mad, to hear herself screaming or laughing uncontrollably.

Nothing happened. The world was quiet again. The sun was warm on the back of her head and on her outstretched arms. She dozed, and remembered the flowers in the churchyard, and seemed to be on the brink of some very simple, very great truth which would explain everything about her own life and about Ben's, about his death and all the life and death of the universe.

She did not know if she had really slept but when she came to herself again, she was rested, there was no longer any confusion or fear. Somehow, somehow, she might yet save herself.

No.

She stood up slowly. Something else had fallen into place. She had no power at all to save herself. And that was the meaning of Friday, and today. Nothing she herself had thought or done or felt since the day of Ben's death had any significance, for feelings were not truth.

She went into the house, where it was cool. Two pieces of knowledge. Ben had had to die, and she had no power to save herself. But the rest of her life was still a tunnel through which she could not yet see any way ahead. She wept again, out of tiredness and longing to have Ben back, to be at an end of this terrible journey before it had begun, she said, 'How can I bear it? How can I go on and on?'

Silence lay upon the air like dust.

Easter passed, the spring flowers withered and were swept off the graves and burned, April went out in a flurry of snow, and in May, the rain began again and Ruth discovered no more truth, only went on, not thinking, not daring to ask for anything at all. And then, at the beginning of July, when she felt that she had lived alone forever and yet could not accept that Ben was dead, the hot, hot days had begun.

PART THREE

10

But she did not go to see Potter the following day;
it took her a week to summon up the courage, and
in that time summer slipped into the beginning of
autumn, as a hand into a familiar glove.

She smelled it first of all, going out of the back
door that morning, to the hens, smelled autumn in the
fine mist, which had condensed and fallen and lay as
a heavy dew, though a few minutes later, the sun was
shafting through, drying out the grass again.

Ruth took a stool and sat outside, patching the
sleeve of a shirt, and heard the first apples thumping
down, though the air did not stir with any breeze;
looked over to the copse, and saw there a hint of yellow about the edges of the glazed treetops, as though
a brush of it had been trailed lightly across. Yesterday,
going over to Rydal's farm, she had seen the last of the
harvesting men, the stubble was ugly as a new-shaven
head, and straw was caught in the hedgerows. Swifts
and swallows gathered and wheeled and turned in
drifts about the sky.

Autumn, she thought, cutting the white cotton.

And did not want it to come, for it was another change, another season to be faced and lived through without Ben. Last autumn ... But she frowned and turned the shirt, roughly, inside out, bent her head, for she would not, would not keep on, going round like a tame mouse on a wheel, remembering.

And so much of the world was green and yellow again, tarnished and dried out, they were not the fresh, sappy colours of spring. There had been so much sun, and the evening brought out clouds of gnats, to dance in a frenzy about her head, and below the branches of the fruit trees.

She did not want autumn, and winter, and the turning of the year. Yet it would be beautiful; the bracken would gradually shrivel and shrink and curl back within itself and yellow would flare up into orange and burn down again, to a darker brown, and the beech woods would change, like the colours of tobacco being slowly, slowly cured.

She thought of the sea, and of a place which might be blue and grey and lavender, of when the woods should be black again and the sun blood-red, and the hills all pillowed out with snow. For this summer had dragged its feet and time had almost stopped and she wanted to be away and knew that she could not.

But she had not thought, this past week, very much about herself. There was no point to it, she had come so far and would carry on, breathe in and out and let her heart beat and that was all. Except for the visit she must make, across the common to where Potter lived, the visit which might confirm or destroy utterly her view of the world.

Her birthday had come and gone, too, she was twenty. And felt a hundred or a thousand years older, all the ages it was possible for a person to be, and also, no age at all, a child damp from the tight, mucoid canal of birth.

Birth and death and resurrection, and one tunnel led into the next.

In the heart of the wood, just before dawn and in the September evenings, a tawny owl called *A-hoo*, and the voices of blackbird and thrush had dropped a tone, the vigour of spring all gone.

She looked at the neat, closely stitched patch on Rydal's shirt and perhaps it was something achieved, something to be a little proud of.

For her birthday, Jo had brought her one of his shells, rare and heavy and curled inwards like a lip, spotted mole brown on a silver-pink skin; and a bunch of tansies and a slab of chocolate and a piece of soapstone carved in the shape of a boat. Looking at him, Ruth had known that his head was awash with the sound of a distant sea, his eyes looked upon some inner vision of masts and sails and moving water. Well then, he might go, for in another year he would finish school and he might choose to follow his great-grandfather Holmes, whose sea trunks he opened almost every day, searching among the treasures. He

might go. She looked up, and let her hands rest on
the shirt. Then, there would be no one, she would be
truly alone.

So it might be.

And I am twenty, she said, and what is that, and
how long may I have yet to live, so that perhaps in
another twenty, or forty or fifty years, I shall not
remember or recognise the person I am now? And
Ben? What of Ben, how shall I meet him, if I am an
old, old woman, how much will he have changed
and grown and moved on? 'Love is not altered by
death.' Yet she thought that now she might prefer it
if she could believe that there would not be the terrible responsibility of another life, she might like to
be blown away and dispersed like smoke on the wind.
She could not choose, for what she knew, she knew.
There were only questions and questions, silting up in
her brain.

Questions.

She stood and folded the shirt neatly and set it
down, for now, she must go, she should not put it off
any longer. It was a quarter past six.

*

What she was thinking, crossing the common on the
rutted path, was that she was twenty years old and
knew nothing. For instance, she said, I never read
books, I know nothing of what great writers have to

say, as Jo does, and as Ben did. And perhaps they might tell me a great deal, teach me and help me, give me some more of the pieces of the puzzle of truth. Or at least I should be taken out of my own thoughts, the days and nights would not be so long. Though she felt that there was virtue to be had in simply enduring.

She remembered poems, two or three, learned at school, by heart and easily, when she was ten or eleven, and recited to her father, and to her father's friends, because he had always wanted to display Ruth to them, he had been proud of her, she might be all that he had to show for fifty years of life.

'Fear no more the heat of the sun,
   Or the furious winter's rages.'

She paused and the words tumbled about like stones confused together in her head, it was an effort to pick them out and lay them in order.

'Golden lads and girls all must,
   Like chimney sweepers, come to dust.'

They had been old poems that she had learned, and sad, they had made her weep, even then, though she had not understood them. She had looked out of the window across the flat fens, at sky and water and reeds, all colourless as bones, and felt close to death.

'I will wash the ploughman's clothes,
I will wash them clean, O,
I will wash the ploughman's clothes,
And dry them on the dyke, O.'

And there had been a tune to that. But she did not
know, even now, why it should have made her cry.

Books. But the books were gone, all those which
had been Ben's at least, shovelled into sacks and loaded
on to the cart of the travelling man, and sold for
money. And where was the money now? Some were
left, her Godmother Fry's books, but only a handful, a
prayer book and a Bible, *The Pilgrim's Progress*, and a
book of receipts, and an English dictionary, *The Life of
Mr. George Herbert*. She had never looked inside them.

'I know nothing.' Perhaps it did not matter.

Potter's cottage, set at the bottom of a slight slope, was
just ahead of her, the roof rose-red in the evening sun.
It was a neat cottage, for a man who lived alone, with
tidy grass and a tidy hedge and fresh paint on gate and
door. Did he cook and clean and wash entirely for
himself, did he have no friends, no visitors at all? She
wondered how lonely he was, and whether he read
books, or thought, or only returned from his work in
the woods, to work on his own garden and walk the
dog and sleep.

She stopped, and half-hid herself behind the brack-
en. Potter. What should she say? And suddenly, her

father and Ellen came into her mind, a picture of them, stripping the fruit from the pear tree, and she realised how long it was since she had seen them, how little she knew of their life together now, and how greatly she herself had changed. They had written, after Ben's death, and asked her to go home, or offered to come here to her, but she would have none of it, she would manage and bring herself through entirely alone. For the truth was that she was afraid, after all those years closed up with her father, in that comfortless house, afraid of being sucked back into the old life, as though she were a child again, so that her time with Ben would be erased and in the end, might never have been. She had broken away and must stay away, they must live without her. And he was married now, he had Ellen, so he should have no more need of her.

There was the chop-chop of a spade striking rhythmically into the earth. He was home, then, and in the garden. She would go. A line of smoke, pencil-thin, streamed up into the air over the top of the hedge, and as she drew nearer the gate, the scent of it pricked in her nostrils, and abruptly, she felt herself swung back hard into the past, and an evening last autumn, when Ben had made a bonfire and it had gusted up at him, filming his face and hair and bare arms with ash. Oh, she thought, oh, this is how it is, it is small things; a bonfire in the evening; this is what makes it so hard to bear. For what she missed now was not passion or important deeds, significant words, but the routine of everyday life, eating and work and sleep and talk of this and that, and the sound of footsteps about the house, the smell of wet boots on the step. Nothing could replace all of this, nothing, though she might live forever. It was not vows and fleshly love and the bearing of children that she wanted, it was so much less, and so much more.

Her hand was on the gate. Yes, the paint was fresh, smooth and rich and shining like new cream, the sun had not had time to blister and dull it down.

She could still go back. She would go back and never speak to him or ask questions, need never hear the truth; she might turn away, now, now, and run, he had not seen her yet. Why had she come at all?

The common was quiet under the sun and it was warm. There was only the regular chop of the spade and the smell of wood-smoke.

She pushed open the gate, went inside and slowly round to the back of the house, and felt that she must have been struck dumb. She saw Potter, his back bent and turned away from her. And realised how much she had let her own garden go wild, for here, everything was flowering and fruiting and clearly in its place, here, the hedge was trimmed and the sunflowers tall as men on stilts, a peach tree was splayed out against the wall. Michaelmas daisies were bunched and tied back, and the vegetable tops sprouted and feathered up, just watered. Here, there was riot and yet very great order. That was how Ben would have had it, given another year, he had worked as hard as Potter was working now, and it had all been allowed to run down to nothing, and that was her fault. She had not even bothered to follow through the little that Jo had managed to do.

He straightened up for a moment and rested one foot on the edge of the spade; not a tall man, and almost white-haired, though he was no more than fifty.

She should go back now. Or else call out, somehow bridge the distance that lay between them, which was the whole of the garden. She could not move. Through a gap she could see the tops of the beeches. Sweat was running down her neck, and clinging to her upper lip, and Potter's shirt was dark with sweat, which had glued it to his back in patches. The sweat of fear and the sweat of work. But why should she be afraid?

She made no sound. Then, the dog Teal came out of the house and barked. Potter looked round. He saw her and called the dog back. They looked at one another, and for a long time, neither of them started forward or spoke, both waited and thought, and remembered; and did not know what was to be done.

The dog sat, obedient but making a small, whimpering noise in the throat, its body quivering. Ruth stretched out a hand and half-called to it, for this seemed a way of breaking the silence between herself and the man, and, knowing it too, Potter murmured to the dog, and it came at once, reassured, trotted quickly to her and let her stroke its head, nuzzled against her. Then, after a moment, it ran back down the garden. She followed it slowly.

'Ruth Bryce,' he said, looking her full in the face questioningly, before glancing down again, at the spade which was half-buried in crumbly soil. 'Ruth Bryce.'

'I – I'd wanted to come. Before this. I meant to come.'

Potter nodded. He had a curious face, the features pressed down together as though a weight lay on top of his head, there were deep lines, one below the other, and fine ones, criss-crossing his forehead like the marks on a map.

She said, 'It's a nice garden,' and felt foolish. But how might she begin?

'Yes.' He took his foot off the spade. 'Yes, it's well enough.'

'We ... I haven't done anything. It's all – there's so much, all the vegetables and flowers, and I don't know about them. It looks so untidy. I haven't done what I should to it.'

'I'd have come. If there was anything. But I didn't like.'

'No.'

'You need help, with the heavy work – the digging.'

'Jo did some – he put up the beans. He's done what he could.'

'Yes.'

'But it's not enough. I shouldn't have let it go.'

'There's time.'

'Yes.'

'You'll find that. There'll be time for it all. In the end.'

'The apple trees – I don't know what to do with those either – there isn't any fruit. Hardly any. They're old – Ben was going to fell them.'

'They were neglected. Left for years.'

The dog Teal was sitting close to Ruth's legs and she bent again and touched its black coat, she thought, perhaps I should have a dog. Perhaps it would be company. Yet she already had the donkey Balaam, and the hens and had scarcely bothered about them since the spring, only done what she must, with food and water. How could she be responsible for a dog?

Potter spoke to it. 'We've a visitor. Eh? We've a visitor.'

The dog thumped its tail.

'I want you to tell me,' Ruth said quickly, before she could lose the courage and make some excuse, run away. 'It's – I want to know. Everything about Ben's death. I've wanted to know but I couldn't ask. Not until now. I want you to tell me.'

'You should know, yes. If it's what you want, you should know.'

The bonfire slipped down in the centre, all the twigs and leaves shifted and sparks went spitting up.

'Making a fire,' Potter said, watching it with her, 'that's a thing I like to do. And in the house, in winter.

It's a thing I can be satisfied with – making up a fire.'

'There's so much here – all the different flowers, things I've never seen before.'

'Herbs,' he said, pointing, 'Miss Fry would have known. They've more scent than a good many flowers. I grow them for the scent – and the show they make. I don't have much use for them.'

She walked over and looked at the fragrant green bushes, marjoram and silvery-grey shaded thyme, and the tall, pale feathery stalks of fennel. She stopped and picked a leaf of mint, rubbed it between her fingers and it was dry and hairy, until the juice was pressed out.

'I'd give you anything you wanted,' Potter said, 'cuttings and plants, for you to make a start. There's nothing to growing those, once they've taken a hold.'

But she turned away, weary, unable to think of planting new things, of making any changes in the garden, unable to put her mind to anything beyond this evening, and the questions she had to ask. Until she knew, all of it, and had accepted what it meant, nothing else could happen. She was on one bank and must cross this river to the other side.

'We'd best go into the house,' Potter said.

And here, too, everything was neat and in order, everything clean. The grate was full of dry logs, laid crossways one on top of the other. Potter went to wash his hands and the chair Ruth sat in was huge and heavy, a man's chair, the room was crammed full of dark pieces of furniture, well-used. She wondered, again, what he did in the evenings and why he had never taken a wife.

Beyond the small windows, the sky was fading and marbled with mulberry-coloured veins of cloud. Well, he must be content, he must not mind the silent house, and only the dog beside him in the room.

He came in, his hands and forearms scrubbed and reddened and the hairs that covered them white as salt.

'Would you take a glass of cider?'

She was aware that he was uneasy, perhaps little used to having strangers in the house, and anxious to make her feel welcome.

'Or tea – I could make you some tea.'

'I'd like to taste the cider.'

'It's good – good and clear. Last year was fine for apples.'

She held the mug he gave her, and felt it cool between her hands; the cider was the colour of honey.

'I get a dry throat, working with wood all day and digging and so on – and then the smoke from the bonfire.'

'It's been hot.'

'Yes. A dry summer.'

'Every day – I get so tired of the sun, everything being parched. I'm tired of the glare of it.'

He nodded, and sat down in the chair opposite her, and the dog stretched itself out on the rug. The cider tasted smooth and sweet in her throat. Potter leaned forwards, hand on his knees, and did not look at her, and she remembered how he had come into the cottage the night of Ben's death and been so concerned about her, and unable to say or do anything in the face of her stubbornness and grief. She felt that now she should make some apology, or thank him, but she could not. She sipped the drink in silence and smelled the smell of apples.

'I'd thought of coming,' Potter said, 'often enough. I'd not like you to feel I hadn't. I've gone past the cottage, taking out the dog.'

'Yes.'

'I'd spoken to the boy. If there'd been anything I could have done ...'

'But there was nothing.'

'No. No.' He glanced at her. 'It stayed with me,' he said, 'I've lived with it every day since.'

She watched him and was ashamed again, for here was someone else about whom she had thought nothing, someone who had known Ben all his life and been close to him, loved him. And how had he borne it? Not only the grief, and the memory of those few hours, when he had been the last person to see Ben alive and the first to see him dead on this earth, but the guilt he must feel, even though the accident had not been his fault. She should have come to him here long ago, said something. But what? How? Oh, she had kept Ben's death to herself, as a private thing, tried to possess it utterly and allow no one else the right to mourn, but it was not here only, for no one lived to themselves alone.

'You were good,' she managed to say at last, 'that night – that day. Good to me. I've never ... I couldn't take it in, not then, but I've remembered it.'

'I worried about you, there on your own, not seeing any one except for the boy. I'd go past and look for a light. I did worry.'

'No one's that strong. Nobody could be. It isn't meant.'

She set down the mug of cider. The shadows lay like fingers over the room, but Potter's white hair and shirt and the bones of his folded knuckles shone.

'Tell me everything, everything that happened. I want to know now.'

'It's time?'

'I've got to know, everything, all the things I can't imagine, all the things I wouldn't let anyone tell me before. I've got to know now.'

'Yes.'

But there was a long silence before he began and she saw his face, and his eyes were far away, looking into the past, she saw how that day had changed him. The dog lay, heavy as stone.

'It was a good day, that. It was fine, clear. I remember looking out, first thing, letting out the dog, and seeing it was going to be a fine day.'

Yes, she thought, as though it had been spring come early. A good day.

'We'd worked down through the slope, clearing out the undergrowth until after dinner. I was with him all the morning, and young Colt up behind us, on his own. Just a day like any other.'

'Did he talk to you? What did he talk about?'

'Not much. He never said much. I worked with him since he was fourteen, we knew each other. But he'd never say a lot.'

'Sometimes he said – oh, strange things.'

'Yes. That day ... he'd often be silent for an hour and then say something you'd not be able to forget. And he never missed anything, he saw whatever went on around.'

'That day?'

'He said – "It's a good life. I've got a good life."'

He bent down and stroked the dog anxiously. Ruth was quite silent. 'A good life.'

'I'd stayed further back, then, up the slope out of sight, and he was down in Helm Bottom. I'd told him to look and see what we could mark out for felling. Rydal was wanting a couple of trees down, big ones, he'd an order for a ton of logs. And there was still a lot of clearing and thinning out to do. It was warm, that day. In the sun. I don't know what I was thinking of. Nothing, I daresay, nothing special. Only enjoying it – I've always been a man who's enjoyed his work. And the good weather.'

He shook his head.

'There was never a sound – nothing, not any warning at all. I'd have known, heard it, and so would he. You get used to what every sound means, and you can tell if a tree's bad and ready to fall, months before. You can see it. Elms – if an elm's rotten the crows don't nest in it. A couple of years ago, on the edge of Great New Common, that row of elms – the crows always nested there, right up high, and then, that time, they left two trees alone. Two, in the centre of that row. It was Ben who saw that, and they were rotten. We had them down. They know, the crows, something tells them. But this one – I'd not seen it, and nor had he. I should have seen it. Rydal didn't think so, he said nothing could have told us. But I should have seen it, after all these years. If I'd looked well enough, I'd have known.'

'Why did it fall just then? Why?'

'The roots spread out underground. When you start on a tree, start up with the axe or the saw, there's a movement and it disturbs everything. And there'd been the gales a few weeks before. But this one – it'd been weakening, anything might have set it off, and the chances were no one would have been near. I shan't ever know what happened, not for certain. I'd heard the axe strike. There's a rhythm to it, everyone has his own. You work to a rhythm. I'd gone further away, up the slope, and there was the noise – just the first sound of strain, but I'd scarcely thought what it was, and the next thing, the sky was falling in, you know, all the weight of a tree crashing down, hitting against others. Crashing down.'

He wiped sweat off his forehead with one finger, and Ruth knew that he was hearing it all over again inside his head, and heard it with him. She knew the noise of a falling tree.

'That was it – but I couldn't seem to move, it was like being struck myself, as though my legs had ... I don't know how long, I don't know – it can't have been long. He'd not shouted out, or else I'd never heard him. It went quiet. Quiet. I was standing stock still in the sun and I didn't need to go down, to look – I felt it happen. It went through me. I felt it. Felt him die. I knew.'

He made a gesture of helplessness, trying to make her understand and believe, and she wanted to tell him that she did, for she had known, too, though she had not been anywhere near. In the garden she was over-whelmed by that knowledge and dread, at the moment of Ben's dying.

'I went down, I ran down, and saw it, saw the tree – where it had broken off, snapped. It was rot-ten through the centre, though the bark looked fresh enough. I should have seen it, I should have known. Months before.'

'No,' Ruth said. 'No.' But he seemed not to hear her.

He said, 'It was like summer in that clearing. Warm as summer.'

He stopped. The dog turned and stretched its legs.

'Tell me,' Ruth said, *'you must tell me.'*

'He was under it, the tree, it had hit him across the back and pinned him down, it was right below his shoulders. He was lying on his face underneath it. He had his arms out. I didn't have to touch him ... I didn't need to.'

'What did you think? Looking at it, at him? What did you think?'

'I thought...'

How could he tell her? For he did not know himself, could not truly describe the silence that had fallen over the whole wood and the way every corner of the air had been seething with the awareness of this sudden death.

'We got it off him – I don't know – somehow. Young Colt had heard, he came running down, and we got it off him between us, dragged it away. But then he was shaken, sick – he's a boy, he'd never seen anything like that, he couldn't ... I knelt down and turned him over. Laid him on his back. I knew, but I had to look, that was only right, I had to be sure, and send for help, even then, in case. Just in case. But I knew.'

'What ...' Ruth picked up the mug of cider and tried to drink from it but her hands were shaking and she had to set it down again.

'Tell me what he looked like, how he was. Tell me that.'

'It had crushed him – crushed his ribs in, and his chest bone.'

'And his head? His face?'

'No. No, only a graze. He'd fallen on to leaves, there was only a bit of a graze on his forehead. Nothing. His eyes were open. I shut his eyes. No, it was just in his chest like ... like something ...'

He clenched his fist tightly.

'And he'd started to bleed, there was blood coming through his shirt and jersey, just coming through. But not his face. Nothing else.'

Ruth closed her eyes and saw Ben lying there, his rib cage and breast bone smashed down into heart and lungs, pressing through the flesh and skin. But not his face, she thought, not his face, or his hands or arms or legs. Nothing else.

'I sent him off – Colt ... off down to the road. Dent was there somewhere, hedging, and then they met Carter, they went off for the doctor ... for the others.'

'But you stayed.'

'I sat by him. Just sat on the ground. On my own with him. It... I've never known it like that. I've never been with death before, seen it come over a man and take him. I've been with it often enough. But I've never felt the same.'

'What? Oh, what?'

'What was true,' he said slowly, 'what was true about it, once and for good. I couldn't doubt the truth, after that. After sitting there with him in the wood. Touching him. It was death and – and life. I'd never doubt that now. Never. It was inside me and all around. And him. A change ... some great change.'

He moved restlessly in his chair. The dog growled through its sleep.

'I can't tell you how it was. I can't make you know it.'

'But I did know. It doesn't matter what's happened since, what I've thought – I've gone over and over it and every day it's been different and I haven't believed it. I haven't believed in God or ... But I knew it that day. I can't pretend I didn't know.'

And then she told him, every detail. About the day before, as she had walked home from Thefton and seen the world transformed, about the rose-quartz and the quiet evening with Ben, and then how it had been, without any warning, in the garden.

'I knew,' she said.

The room was quite dark now.

'Where did they take him? Who took him? Who touched him?'

'The doctor – Doctor Lewis from Thefton. We moved him, after the doctor had done. I lifted him up myself – with Carter. We carried him down to the lane and put him into the trap. That was all. There was nothing else for us to do after that.'

'And then everyone heard about it, everyone knew, the Bryces and all the village, everyone ... But I knew it first. I knew the same moment. How did I know?'

'It happens. Things happen between two people.'

Ruth said, 'I didn't see him ... when he was dead. They all saw him, at the house, they went up and stared at him. And I didn't. I was afraid. I didn't want to see what he looked like. I wish I had now.'

'But you've got what you need, to remember. You have that, Ruth.'

'If I'd seen him … You said it wasn't his face?'

'I've told you the truth. You've a right to know it. I've told you how it was.'

'I don't want to have my feelings spared.'

'You've not had that.'

'No.' She looked at Potter. 'And now…'

She was aware of a change in the room, because at last, there was the truth, and nothing left to know and because she had shared it with him and she saw exactly how it had been for him, too. Something lay between them like a fine thread which could never break. Potter. He had held on to all this knowledge, all these truths and memories and feelings, kept them for her until she was ready to receive them.

'Now …' But she did not know what she could say about now, about the present or the future, about Ben, about herself. And his body had been lying on the ground, the life crushed under the weight of the fallen tree, and the blood staining his clothes and seeping away into the soil. *But not his face.*

Without any warning, the tears rose up and broke out of her, and Potter sat on his chair, saying nothing, and yet being a comfort to her, taking some of her grief on to himself. She wept as she had never wept before in front of any human being and it was a good thing to do, it was of more value than all the months of solitary mourning. It brought something else to an end.

*

Potter prepared a meal for them both, cold beef and bread and pickles, and although Ruth said she could eat nothing, when she tasted the pink, moist meat, she found that she was ravenously hungry. Potter watched her.

'You should eat. It's not good to neglect yourself. It's not what he'd have wanted.'

And she was not angry or resentful, as she had been at the beginning, when people had told her what Ben would have said or thought or wanted. Potter was right and she accepted it and the concern which had made him speak.

She looked down at her empty plate. This was the first time that she had shared a meal with anyone at all, even Jo, since Ben's death. Somehow, Potter had brought her out of herself, though he had not talked very much, after he had finished the story of that day. She wanted to ask him, now, whether he minded being alone here, how he lived, for perhaps there was some secret that he might teach her, a knack to it. It was how her own life would be, and for good, she was sure of that. She would be alone, and must make the best of it. But she could not bring herself to pry, as others might, and she feared to offend him.

She got up. She would go home, she said, and he walked with her over the common, the dog bounding away ahead of them.

'I'm glad I came. I'm glad you told me – told me all of it.'

'You've to live with it now. It won't be something you can forget.'

'I don't want to forget.'

'If I'd not told you the truth, you'd have imagined worse.'

'Yes.'

Oh, and she had, she had, her dreams, waking and sleeping, had been full of the sight of Ben, with his face crushed and broken, altogether changed, and dying slowly under the weight of the tree, screaming out in pain, alone. Well, it had not been as bad as that and perhaps she could live with the truth.

Potter said, 'I'll look out for you. When I go by, I'll look out.'

But she knew that he would never intrude.

He called back the dog, and she stood just inside the gate hearing his footsteps go away. It was a warm night and clear, and as she looked up, she remembered that Ben had tried to teach her about the stars, had told her their names. He said, 'It's easy. It's like a town you get to know – streets you could walk through. When you've looked often enough, it's easy.'

But the pattern of the sky had never been clear to her, each night the stars seemed to have shifted their places, they were like flowers strewn about anyhow in a meadow. She had liked their names. Ben had written some of them down for her and she had spoken them aloud to herself, for pleasure.

Perseus. The whirlpool. Nebula. Ursa Major. Auriga, the Charioteer. Eridanus, the river. Camelopardum. The Pleiades...

Yet even as a small child, she had not believed, as others did, that heaven was in the stars, up and up above her, for there was something that frightened her in the night sky, a coldness, with only air rushing through the dark spaces between. No, she had always sensed that heaven was no further away than the tips of her own fingers, and if she were given eyes to see, it would be there, all about her and astonishingly familiar. She felt it now. If she reached out

She dropped her hand to her side. She could not do it. She could only wait, live her life as best she might. And today had been important, something had been achieved, some step taken.

She went down the garden to put away the hens.

11

She wondered sometimes if she had been alive at all, during those years before she met Ben. For it seemed that he had taught her all she knew, and she had depended upon that and never doubted or questioned what he told her, she had had no cause to think independently. And now she must. But still, as autumn spread out its hands and covered the countryside, everything she saw and heard and recognised and knew by name, had come from Ben. She supposed that she must have been aware of the changed time and weather, from season to season, during the years at home with her father, but she could remember nothing of them, the flat land and sky and estuary had only been a pale backdrop to her everyday, closed-up life. Coming here, she had been born into a new world, she had gained the use of eyes and ears, had discovered how to smell and taste and touch. Some said that only in childhood were all the senses free and sharp, but that had not been true for her. She had been a chrysalis muffled in an opaque, papery shroud and it was Ben who had awakened her.

After the evening with Potter, she slipped back again into that slow rhythm of living, which she had grown used to since the late spring; she slept and worked and ate alone, and the days passed, each so like the last that she could not tell whether it was Monday or Friday. But she was rested, she no longer wept for part of every single day and night, though tears would still overtake her abruptly in the middle of doing some job, while she was not even consciously remembering or missing Ben.

She was not happy, but neither was she truly unhappy. She existed. And the colours and sounds changed, the evenings drew in a little like shadows and the early morning smelled raw, at night, it was cold.

Jo came, walking all the way up to the cottage from school, but not every day now. She saw no one else, except the man who brought the sewing from Rydal, and Potter once or twice, as he passed by the gate, or went over the common with the dog, and paused, looked for her and lifted his stick in greeting. But he did not come near.

The trees darkened to rust and brown, or paled to topaz yellow, though some lingered, a dull green. Hips and haws reddened in the hedgerows, and on the common and along the lanes the blackberries ripened slowly to the colour of wine, and sloes to slate and indigo blue. She thought of all the things she might do – gather crab apples and strain them to make jelly, and sloes for gin, buy windfall pears from Rydal and bottle them. During the two previous autumns, Ben had taught her what to look for, which fruits to gather and when, and how to transform them into the juices and jams, clear and thick in their glass jars. But she only picked a handful of blackberries now and then, and ate them raw, spitting out those which were still hard and sour. For where was the point of taking the basket and filling it and spending hours in the kitchen, where there would be no one but herself to eat and enjoy what she made, through the coming winter? She supposed that she might sell things and make a little more money. But she did not.

She sat in the garden or walked across the fields and into the wood, which was very still, very dark and smelling of decay, she went down as far as the river and stared into it and all through these days, felt that she was the still centre of a disintegrating world. Birds gathered and fell in flocks down through the sky like confetti, ready to fly south, others, the bramblings and fieldfares, would come; bevies of lapwings and partridge followed the plough as it turned over the soil of the fields and left it brown. There was no longer any singing, only the low, peevish chatter of jays and magpies. Wood pigeons huddled silent among the dying trees and grasshoppers hid in silence, close to the ground.

But still, in the middle of the day, the sun shone,

it was warm and dry, and the farmers and gardeners were uneasy, the cattle inert, prayers were said in the church for rain.

12

But always, it was the woods which drew her, she rarely walked in the open fields now, or up and over the ridge, and as September ripened and trailed away into the next month, the air that hung about the trees was close and still and there was a slow fermentation of leaves and soil and fruits and fungus, a dampness which came from mists and dew, but which seemed rather to be sweat forced out of pores in the bark. She was half-afraid of the sweet smell of decay, and the silence everywhere. But as the first leaves dried up and fell, there were gaps through which the sun shone, as in early spring, and sycamore wings came spinning slowly down the beams of light.

The heavy sleep of the early weeks after Ben's death had given way to disturbed restless nights, when she seemed always to be just on the brink of consciousness and disconnected images and sounds streamed through her head. She got up early, and looked at herself in the glass and saw fine, pale patches beneath her eyes, though her skin was tanned after all the days of sun. She said, I am older. And indeed, her face had altered, the roundness and blurred outlines of child-hood were sharpening, her bone structure was defined. Was twenty old or young? She could not tell.

Now, she turned over in bed and opened her eyes and the room was still dark, but she knew that she would not sleep again, and although the air was cold, her skin, and sheets and blankets seemed to be burn-ing. She got up and went to the window, and saw that it was that dead time between the end of night and the beginning of morning.

She went out. Silence. Stillness. It was what she was so used to, she was never afraid; though why she needed to come out like this and walk down through the lanes and into the woods alone, she did not know, for it tired her, the country was cold and lifeless, she saw nothing, heard nothing, except the sound of her own footsteps and the beating of her own heart. It was a change, though, from the dryness of heat and bright-ness of the daytime, she could think more clearly.

She went first to Helm Bottom, feeling her way through to the clearing and the fallen elm. Its surface had changed now, soft, spongy fungus had crept over the dead bark, and insects were hidden in the crevices and ran lightly over her hands and in between her fin-gers. There was a fetid smell.

Death, she thought. For she was surrounded by it, and it was not sudden death, a clean severing of body and soul, as Ben's death had been; it was slow, stealthy death. What had been growing and full of sap, sprouting and erect, taking over the world, had been overcome and was shrivelling back within itself, there was mould and corruption and fading, things dried and fell, and were gradually blotted up by the moisture from the earth. There had been spring and there would be winter. But then spring again. Death and a new life. She could feel both within herself, as though the old blood was drying out, and giving way to new, though the process had hardly begun. It was change, and she could only let it overtake her, without knowing what might be to come, what emotions and beliefs and experiences would replace those of the past. But they could only grow up out of the soil of that past. So everything had been necessary.

There was a paleness at the edges of the wood, and she sat waiting, as it spread and reached her, so that she could just see the silvery trunks of the surrounding trees. She got up and went on down towards the stream. It had almost dried up, the trickle of water scarcely moved and the stones were silted over with a fine mud.

She wondered how long she would drift, and feel weary, in the heat of the day, and come out here, to sit for hours, or walk slowly between the trees, what would eventually break the pattern and waken something new in her, some desire or hope, and give her the energy to pursue it. There were times when she blamed herself and believed that no change could come about unless she herself willed it and sought after it; and times when she knew that she could do nothing but wait, for something to come from outside and shake her alive.

Certainly, until now she had brought about no real developments in her life by any exercise of her own will; things had happened to her, and she had accepted that, and could not tell if it had been right or wrong, good or bad. She was afraid of taking any initiative with time and circumstance, people and places. She had never done so, because her father had been there, and Ben. No, she would be still, she would simply wait.

The stones of the stream were whitening and the water took on a slight sheen under the strengthening light. And then she heard it, the voice of a man, somewhere behind her in the wood, heard a desperate, broken calling out and sobbing. She did not move, though she was not afraid. But who else would ever come here in the early hours of the morning, to stumble and then halt, then grope forwards again, and all the time letting out such cries, of anger or pain or distress? Who?

She waited by the stream, thinking that the man might come upon her. It had grown a little lighter and then the dawn had settled back on itself, to a greyness, mid-way between dark and day. There was no sun.

The footsteps stopped but the crying went on, muffled now, and coming from somewhere up the slope. It was a harsh noise, with, occasionally, a rasp of breath, in and out. It reminded Ruth of something.

Yes, of her own ugly weeping, during those early days and nights.

She began to search. But when, eventually, she did come upon him, she stopped dead, shocked and not daring to go nearer, not understanding. It was Ratheman, the curate. He was sitting on the ground, his knees drawn up and his back bent over, his head down. He was sobbing and clenching and opening his fists over and over again, and his hair was tangled and wild, anyhow about his head. He was muttering something, too, but his words were choked and garbled together, she could not make them out. He had not heard Ruth and she stood there for a long time, anxious and without any idea of what she might do. She noticed that his clothes were crumpled as though he had slept in them, and the trousers were stained with damp, and torn here and there, as they had snagged against briars and branches. She had never in her life seen a man cry. She wanted to go away. But how could she? He was half-mad with some terrible grief, she could not simply walk off and leave him alone. And in the end, she took a few steps forwards. He did not move. A fine rain had begun to drift down.

She said, 'What is it? Oh, what is it?'

Though her voice was scarcely more than a whisper.

For a moment after he looked up, she knew that he did not see her, did not know where he was or why. His eyes stared, and they were swollen and red, his face was trammelled with lines of tears. He looked strange, and old, though he was not old. He was not wearing his clerical collar and his neck looked white and dead, as flesh which had never before been exposed to the daylight. He began to shudder, and then shook his head violently. And looked up at Ruth again. He was kneeling, but in silence now. She went up to him. Knelt down.

'I heard you. I was by the stream and I heard you ... what is it?'

He continued to watch her face blankly, and made no effort either to speak, or to wipe his eyes and face. He was huddled up like an animal or a child in great pain. The thin rain was falling without making any sound, but his hair and the shoulders of his coat were beaded with it. Ruth thought, we prayed for rain and here, at last, is an end to the dryness and the endless shining of the sun. She reached out and touched the man's sleeve.

'Shall you come home? It's raining. It's only six o'clock in the morning. Shall I go home with you?'

And, hearing herself, she realised that she was saying those things which other people had once said to her, and they had made her angry, but now she understood how the words and questions had had to be spoken out, for they were offerings, attempts to share and soften her grief. And she had rejected them.

'What are you doing here? You? Why are you here?' He spoke harshly.

'I – I often come. I wake up and come out to walk.

It's quiet. I usually come here, into the wood. And I heard you. Are you ill?'

He shivered again.

'Did you hear what I was saying?'

'No. It wasn't clear. You were crying out but I couldn't tell the words.'

'Crying out. Yes. I was ...'

He was very quiet now, and there was no expression in his voice. The rain was falling more heavily, pattering down through the leaves.

'You shouldn't sit here. It's wet. Not here.'

'No.' But he did not move. He said, 'My daughter is dead. Yesterday she was ill, and today she is dead. Today she is dead.'

His daughter. She remembered that Carter had told her, a few weeks ago -when was it? – of the birth of a second child to the curate's wife. And there was the other, small girl, perhaps three years old, with very clear, pale skin. Ruth did not even know her name.

'My daughter is dead.'

And then he struggled to his feet and stood and shouted out, so that the whole wood rang with it, he raved like a man demented.

'She is dead, and where are you now, God, where is all your love and goodness, when she was in pain and there was nothing to ease it, and now she is dead, and what do you know of it, what do you care? What have I got left? Why didn't you kill me, why not me?

Wouldn't I have been glad of it? But my child is dead and I ...'

The shouting faltered and ceased. He looked up, through the canopy of fading leaves, to the patches of sky. Ruth thought, something will happen to him, he will be struck down. A tree will fall. The sky will fall. And she felt a moment of pure terror, fear for the man and fear of him.

Nothing happened. The rain fell. And Ratheman began to weep again, covering his face with his hands.

'God forgive me,' he said, 'Oh, God forgive me.'

Ruth stood up then and took his arm gently, and he did not resist. She led him down through the slope of the woods and across the meadow and out into the lane, and all the way back to the village, and the rain came steadily down from a dirty sky, soaking her clothes through to the skin. He followed her like a child, walking blindly, still weeping. She knew that she must help him. She prayed.

13

There were no lights on and the house was silent. Ruth stood just behind Thomas Ratheman in the dark, wood-panelled hall and the rain dripped from her hair down on to her shoulders and from the hem of her dress on to the floor. She had never been here before, she scarcely knew these people, and what should she do now, go or stay? Ratheman seemed not to be aware of her presence at all.

A draught blew under the front door. And then, from upstairs somewhere, the hungry, demanding cry of a baby.

She said, 'You should take off your wet things.'

He turned and stared at her, looked puzzled.

'Your wife – is she upstairs or…?'

But she realised that he had not taken in what she said, and still did not know where he had been or why, what had happened.

He walked away from her, opened a door and closed it behind him, and then there was silence again, apart from the distant crying.

It was a large house, and old, and the carpet on the

staircase ahead of her was worn away in patches here and there. Ben had told her how poor a curate could be, but she was shocked, all the same, by the shabbiness and the air of neglect about this place. It might have belonged to old, old people who kept half the rooms shut up and empty, and could not pay for servants or very much coal; there seemed to be no light or life here.

The baby went on crying, so that, in the end, she made her way slowly up the stairs and along a corridor, calling out Mrs. Ratheman's name as she went. There was no reply, nor any when she knocked twice on the door of the room from which the crying came. She went inside.

The curtains were half-drawn back and the windows smeared with rain, so that for a moment she could not see very clearly inside. She stood, holding on to the door handle, and twisting it nervously.

'What is it?'

She was lying in bed, propped on a pillow, with her fair hair in plaits over her shoulders. Mrs. Ratheman. A young woman, perhaps not much older than Ruth, but with eyes and mouth strained and drawn downwards by exhaustion and shock. Ruth remembered someone saying that, since the birth of the second child, she had never been completely well. Now, she looked at Ruth without surprise or much interest.

'What is it?'

From a cot beside her bed, the crying grew louder,

and the mother turned her head on the pillow and looked down, but did not speak to the baby or attempt to pick it up.

Ruth took a step further into the room. But she wished that she had not come here at all, for what could she do or say? What did this woman think of her?

'It cries. It cries so much. I can't bear the way it always cries.'

'Can I get something for her? Or lift her up?'

'It cries all the time. Isobel never cried. Hardly ever. Do you know, all day yesterday, when she was so ill, she didn't cry at all? And now she's dead and can't cry. You knew she was dead? Isobel?'

'Yes, I met your husband. I was out walking in the wood and... and he was there. He told me. I brought him home.'

'You're Ben Bryce's widow.'

'Yes.'

'Why did you come here?'

'To see ... I thought Mr. Ratheman should come home. It was raining. It didn't seem right for him to be wandering about, he was so upset, and ... I thought there might be something I could do.'

'What can you do?'

'Nothing,' Ruth said quietly, 'nothing.'

'No. You'd know that. There's nothing anyone can do.'

'Perhaps...'

'What?'

'I could make a meal – or see to the baby. I could help.'

'Why should you?'

'But perhaps you'd rather I went away. You won't want strangers.'

'Where has my husband gone?'

'He's downstairs. He went into one of the rooms.'

'He cried, do you know that? All last night. He didn't go to bed, he didn't undress. He sat in that chair and wept and couldn't find anything to say to help himself, and I couldn't help him. But I didn't weep. I should be the one to weep, but I didn't. They cry, my husband and the baby. Isobel never cried, not even when she was very small, do you know that?'

'You told me.'

But the young woman went on, talking very rapidly, as though afraid of what might happen if she stopped, afraid of silence.

'When she was a baby, and she was hungry, she just opened her eyes; she whimpered sometimes, when her gums were sore, but I could pick her up and talk to her, and then she stopped, it was easy to make her quiet and sleep. And yesterday...'

She shifted about in the bed, stirred her arms and legs so that the faded pink quilt slipped a little to one side.

'She said, "My head hurts, my head hurts." But she didn't cry, not at all. I wouldn't have known that she was ill. Not really ill. It was Tom – he knew. She was more his child, she was close to him, and he knew. Her eyes looked strange, she kept putting her hand over them. She said, "My head hurts." And she was so hot, you could put your hands over her cot and feel the heat coming from her. That was when the doctor came. But she was dying, he said so, she had a brain fever – something, nobody could help her, it was nobody's fault. I couldn't bear it, sitting there, watching her, waiting for her to die, I didn't stay. He stayed. He sat by her all day, and the baby cried and cried. It always cries. But Isobel didn't cry and then she died. One minute she was alive and breathing and then she was dead. Nobody could help her. It was nobody's fault.'

She sat up suddenly and shouted out at the baby, 'Oh stop, stop, why can't you stop? I can't stand it – cry, cry, cry.'

Ruth crossed the room and picked the child up. It was quiet at once, and gazed up at her, its eyes dark as acorns. She sat in a chair and rocked it a little. And looked across, at the young mother, lying in the high bed. But she had turned away, on to her side, with one of the thick plaits of hair covering her face, and after a while, she slept, and so Ruth sat on, with the baby in her arms, until it slept, also, and then there was only the rain to watch as it streamed down the window.

*

She did not know exactly how it came about that she stayed with them for the whole of the following week. Nothing was said, she was not asked to be there, or to do the work, but after that first morning, when she bathed and changed the baby, and then lit the range in the kitchen and took down the shutters and cooked breakfast, they simply came to rely upon her completely, as she had relied upon Jo. She did the washing and ironing, cooked and cleaned the house, knowing that if she did not, everything would be left.

Ratheman's wife would get up in the middle of the day, and dress and then sit, staring out of the window on to the garden. Or else, more often, she would follow Ruth about the house, talking, talking, about the dead child, Isobel, and the endless crying of the baby, repeating the same words in desperation, as though Ruth had not yet understood. And Ruth grew afraid of her, of the wild, and distant expression in her eyes and the monotonous, hysterical voice. She wondered if Miriam Ratheman had been ill even before Isobel's death, not only in body but in her mind. She was withdrawn, even while she talked, her whole attention was focused on some point deep inside her own self, and the flood of speech was like an issue of blood she could not control, was not even aware of.

She would come to Ruth and stand helplessly in front of her, would ask, 'Should I eat now? Should I change my dress? Is it time to bath the baby?' and then wait like a small child to be given instructions. Ruth became used to it, and would reply, but it was strange, frightening, to be so depended upon.

The curate himself she scarcely saw. But what shocked her most of all was how little contact there seemed to be between husband and wife, how little they noticed each other's existence in the house. He sat in his study, with the door locked, or else went out, walking for hours on end, to return, exhausted and pale, with his clothes damp or torn, and then he would eat whatever Ruth had cooked for him, but without seeming to know what it was. People came, and he would not see them. And so Ruth realised at last how she herself had been, and how it had seemed to others, when she had shut herself away, or spent hours in the woods, or beside Ben's grave at night, all sense of time lost.

And, just as she had visited the grave, Ratheman would go up to the small bedroom in which his dead child lay, and sit beside her, thinking perhaps that he might somehow be given the power to bring her to life again.

Ruth had avoided that room. But on the day before the funeral, as she was drying her hands after washing up the crockery, she knew that she must go up there, now, at once, that she must see and should not run away.

As she touched the door-handle, she felt a tightness in her chest and throat, and wondered how she could breathe. But she must see. She went inside slowly.

He was sitting with his head in his hands, weeping. Ruth moved towards the bed, which was beside the window. He did not notice her. She looked down.

She thought, so this is death. This. This is Ben, and Godmother Fry, and every other person in the world who has ever lived, and breathed and then ceased to breathe. This is the body, after the spirit has left it. She put out a hand and touched the child, and the skin felt cold and smooth, like fruit. But there was peace in this room, peace and a sense of inevitability, for the small girl looked as though she had never been destined to grow and change. She had come just so far. That was all.

But how would she have felt if it had been her child, conceived by Ben and delivered out of her own body? Would not this death then have seemed to her an utterly evil thing? She could not tell. She could only look on at the grief and despair of the father, and at the mother's madness, and understand how it was for them, know how far they had to go, and feel pity.

The young man lifted his head. He was unshaven and his flesh looked curded, as if it had even less life in it than that of the child.

'Why?' he said. 'Why? Why do other people live, old people, sick people, bad people, when she is dead? Why don't they die? Why?'

Ruth was silent.

'Don't you wonder that, too? You should, oh, you should. Why did your husband die? What sort of justice was that? And I prayed. I prayed for a miracle, for her to be well and live, and after she was dead, I prayed for her to be raised up again. But she is dead. She is still dead.'

'Yes.'

'And tomorrow I have to carry her in a coffin and lay her in the ground. How can I do that? How can I let her go?'

'You must.'

His face crumpled, as though she had struck a blow to it, he turned away from her, and bent down over the bed, and began to sob again, but loudly now, out of anger and resentment.

Ruth left him, for there was nothing at all that she could say to help him.

She went back to the kitchen, and began to wash the baby's clothes, and outside the window, the sun shone on to the grass and a blackbird hopped and hopped about, its feathers glistening like washed coal.

*

Ruth was sitting alone in the rocking chair, beside the kitchen window, when he came looking for her.

She wanted to go home now, to be alone again, for this week with the Rathemans had tired her out. There had been the work, her body ached at the end of each day, even though Carter's wife had come in two mornings, to help with the cleaning. But it was their grief and distress which had exhausted her most of all, she felt as though they had sucked her down into it, asked her to share it with them, at times, even, to carry it for them altogether, and she was not ready, her own misery and bewilderment and loss were still upon her, she was still trying to work out her own salvation.

She needed the empty cottage, and time and space for her own thoughts, the slow process of her own recovery, though she felt ashamed of this selfishness.

She had not been to the child's funeral, but stayed with Miriam Ratheman, who had lain in her bed all the day, and was either still and silent, or asleep, or else sitting up, talking in odd fragmented sentences, scarcely pausing for breath, and making no sense, her eyes intent all the time upon Ruth's face.

From the window, Ruth had watched the curate leave the house, carrying the coffin in his arms. How must that have felt to him? She had said again, God help them. But did not know how it might be.

Now, he said, 'They're asleep. They are both asleep and I feel as if I shall never sleep again. I wanted the doctor to see her, but she won't have anyone. I don't know if she is really ill, if she's out of her mind. I can't tell. I can't do anything for her.'

'Could any doctor help her?'

For it seemed to Ruth that what had been true for her would be so for Ratheman and his wife, that they had to make the journey through their own grief, and there was no medicine which could ever help them.

'I came to thank you,' he said.

'There's no need.'

'I must thank you.'

He had been speaking formally, politely, but now, suddenly, he shouted out at her, 'What are you doing this for? Why are you here with us? Haven't you seen enough of death and suffering?'

Yes, she thought, yes. But did not answer him. After a moment, he sat down heavily on one of the upright wooden chairs.

He said, 'I should leave here. I should resign from Holy Orders and go away from this place. What right have I to stay now?'

'Because your child died?'

'Because she has died and now I know that everything I believed in and lived for has died with her. Because my life is a lie. I am a lie. How can I visit them, people sick, people dying and in distress, needing truth, what have I to say to them? How can I take services in the church and preach and pray and know that it is all a lie? I used to know what words to say, but there are no words, and there is no help for anyone. I think of how I went to people and talked to them, about death and goodness and consolation, and I feel ashamed, I knew nothing, I had never felt what they felt. I read books and learned lessons and thought I understood. But it was a lie. How can I stay here?'

Ruth said slowly, 'Things change. They seem different. After a time, they are different.'

Though these were only words, too, and she did not know how he could follow her meaning, because it was so unclear even to herself.

'But it was the same for you. I know it. You shut yourself away, you wouldn't see me, or anyone, and at his funeral, you didn't weep. I saw you in the church-yard at night, lying beside his grave, and what were you thinking then? What could anyone have said to you? I saw well enough how it was, and now I know myself. I blamed you. I don't blame you now.'

'But there were some days ... after he died ... some days, it was easier. There were things I seemed to understand.'

He shook his head violently.

'How could there be anything to understand? There was no meaning to it. Your husband was young and fit, and a good man, he was happy, you were happy, and then he was dead, and now my child is dead, and there is only cruelty, there is no purpose in any of it. It means nothing.'

Ruth rubbed the cloth of her skirt between her fingers, afraid of the violence of his despair, and the bitterness in his voice, and shocked, too, for she had thought that a priest must surely know more, be able to understand and explain more than any other person.

She began to try and tell him about the way the world had looked changed and altogether beautiful, sometimes, how, here and there, without warning, it seemed that she had been given some brief glimpse of the pattern of things; told him what she had felt at the funeral, and what Potter had felt, as he had knelt beside Ben's body in the wood. And Ratheman gazed at her, and she saw that nothing she had said held any meaning for him, that she had no right at all to speak, there was no comfort for his own loss.

He said, 'Everything is broken into pieces and no one can fit them together again. Why? Why?'

But how could she know?

'My father was a priest, and his father, too, there was never any question about it – that it was what I would be. My father was a good man, and I thought I should be like him. Before he died, he was very ill, for months, he grew weaker and thinner, he had more and more pain, but it was so slow. He kept on, trying to work, taking the services, visiting people because they relied on him but, in the end, he couldn't even read. And yet it took so long for him to die, even when he asked to die. I came home – I was at the university and they sent for me – I can't forget how he looked. I didn't recognise him. He was shrivelled, it was as though he had no flesh left, you could just see bones, showing through the skin. His skin was yellow. He looked so old. He couldn't eat anything. My mother sat with him and gave him sips of water, that was all. And then, one night, we thought he was dying, and I sat with him. And he said, "I always believed. But now I know." But what has happened to me? I do not believe, and I know nothing. Why do I have to live at all?'

He put his head down on to the table and was still, too tired and despairing even to weep, now.

'And you, Ruth? What will you do, for the rest of your life?'

'I don't think about the rest of my life now. I used to – I would be with Ben. Now I don't know.'

'Why don't you go away?'

'Where should I go to?'

'How can you bear it, staying there in that house, going into those woods, remembering?'

'Going away wouldn't make me forget.'

'The Bryces ...'

'I don't see them. Except Jo. The Bryces are strangers.'

'Everyone is a stranger.'

'But you still have your wife. And another child.'

'I want Isobel. The only thing I want, I don't have.'

'No.'

'*What will happen to me?*'

She thought, what will happen to any of us? But she was still afraid of him, as she was of his distracted wife, she felt threatened by them, for her own world was still so frail, it was as much as she could do to cling to that and hold it together.

'I should go home tomorrow.'

'Yes. Of course.'

But seeing the expression on his face, she was more than ever ashamed.

'Isn't there someone else who could be here? To

look after you – to help your wife. Is there no one at all?'

He passed a hand over his forehead.

'My sister ... or ... I don't know. Yes. Someone. I'll think of someone.'

I ought to stay, she thought, I have no reason for running away, I ought to help them. Oh, but she could not, she could not.

'Will you eat something now?'

'No.' He stood up. 'No.' And went out of the kitchen. She heard the door of his study close and the key turn in the lock.

Upstairs, Miriam Ratheman and the baby were both asleep still. Ruth drew the curtains and went out.

She left the house very early the following morning. She could go into the cottage and close the door, and then she would be alone, and responsible for no one but herself, she would be free to hold on to herself, and weep again for Ben, and remember.

'And you, Ruth? What will you do for the rest of your life?' Well, perhaps she would only do this.

Up on the common, the air was very cold, and smelled of the first frost; the world was slipping down towards winter, to bare branches and high winds beating down the bracken, and the late mornings and long nights of dark.

14

She stood at the window, looking out to where the hawthorn and holly bushes were hung about with clots of berries, orange as fire, red as blood. She took a deep breath, held it within herself, let it go softly, she thought, I am myself. And saw someone passing the hedge, walking very slowly, a woman, her head, with her hair covered by a blue scarf, just visible over the tangled mesh of twigs. Who would be coming here? Ruth remembered the curate's wife, and felt a rush of anxiety and guilt, realising clearly now that she had been very wrong, for the woman was ill, it was surely more than grief for her dead child which caused her to behave as she did, to talk wild nonsense and stare in terror ahead of her, to lie sleeping in exhaustion for hour after hour, and dread the sound of her own baby's crying. And she had been asking, as well as she could, for some sort of help from Ruth, a way out of the trap, she wanted someone to come and heal her storming mind and sick body, and Ruth had done nothing, Ratheman did nothing, he was withdrawn into his own grief, and helplessness, preoccupied with his own doubts. What would they do now, alone together in that house, husband and wife and yet as far apart as people in different worlds? Who was there to go to them and take up the baby, bathe and talk to it, make it laugh?

She said, it is not my fault, their troubles are not mine. I did what I could. She closed her eyes.

And, opening them, she saw the young woman coming down the front path, her face swollen and pale as a mistletoe berry, and one hand held up in an odd, defensive position over her breast. But it was not Ratheman's wife, it was Alice Bryce. Alice, who had always frightened Ruth, and repelled her, who had been scornful and distant, unsmiling. Well, she did not smile now. But she was changed, there was a vacant expression on her face, as though she had just suffered a shock, or some accident. She did not see Ruth watching her from the window. And it was a long time before she knocked, not loudly, upon the door.

Alice Bryce. Why had she come here, to break open the bubble of solitude and quietness Ruth had just settled into, to bring the smell of the past and old quarrels and resentments, to remind her that Ben had belonged to others, long before she herself had known him? She had nothing to say to Alice. So perhaps she would simply not go to the door, she would run upstairs and wait until the girl went away. Apart from Jo, the family had made no attempt to see her, nor did she want them, as far as they were concerned, she was as dead to them as

Ben was dead, they need not concern themselves with one another. 'Strangers,' she had said to Ratheman.

The knocking had ceased, but Alice did not go away. Well, the day had been soured now. She would open the door.

Ben's sister was sitting on the step, with her back to Ruth. A wind had risen, and blew in gusts over the common, shifting the tops of the trees and tossing down dead leaves. Alice turned her head. Did not get up.

She said, 'There wasn't anything else I could do. I was going to wait until you came back. Do you think I wanted to come here, if there'd been anywhere else?'

She looked ill, but there was all the old hostility in what she said and in the tone of her voice, the way she held herself. Yet Ruth thought that, now, she was using it as a defence.

'I've been at the curate's house. Their daughter died.'

'Jo said.'

'Someone had to help them.'

'Someone usually does. In the end.'

Alice stood up and faced Ruth, looked into her face for a long time, without speaking again, so that Ruth felt as she had always done with her, and with Dora Bryce, too, uneasy and inferior, but also angry, determined not to let them break her down. They did not like her, they did not try to hide it. She wondered if one kind word had ever passed between any of them.

But something else had changed. Alice, who had been her mother's hope and pride, the one who was allowed to sit about, who was waiting for the chance Dora Bryce had never had, Alice, on whom so much time and praise and money, though never love, had been lavished, Alice was not only tired or ill, she was untidy, and even dirty, her hair, under the cotton scarf, was dull, and the collar of her dress creased. Down her left cheek were faint, strawberry-coloured smears, as though she had been scratched or struck. So she was vulnerable, then, after all, she was not exceptional, or very beautiful or rare.

They went on looking at one another, and the wind blew, banging the gate hard. Ruth stepped back and opened the door wider, for her sister-in-law to come in.

*

The voices sought him and found him out, he could not escape from them, even though he was shut away here in his own room at the top of the house, they rang through the walls and floorboards, the shouting and the anger were more than he could bear; his mother's voice was shrill and repetitive, as the mynah bird he had once heard, as it sat on a man's shoulder at Thefton market. Then she wailed, as she had done through all those days and nights after Ben's death, and Alice would interrupt her, the short, scornful words chopping down like knives; and below it all, the dull, patient rumble of his father, trying to keep the peace between them. Though Jo could not remember when there had ever been any real peace in this house. There was only, sometimes, an uneasy quiet which lay about the rooms, like a sea waiting to rise up again into storm.

He lay on his bed, listening, and the voices were like instruments in some terrible orchestra, all at odds with one another, all clashing. When Ben was here, it had been better, Ben had been able to quieten them, not so much by what he said, but just by his presence among them, because he himself was quiet.

Jo forced his fingers hard into his ears, until the narrow, bony tunnels were sore, he tried to read his book again, one of the diaries he had found in his great-grandfather's trunk, tried to make pictures and hear sounds in his own head which would drown everything else.

'September 9 We have had calm now for the past seven days, as though this were our reward, after the rigours and afflictions we endured in the terrible gales of last month. The crew have borne up well and I thank God we have water enough, and no more cases of the dysentery, which took such a toll of the men.

September 11 We are at anchor in the small creek at the far westerly point of this group of islands, and have before us a sight of the most amazing and refreshing beauty. A rich green of vegetation, fresh and more vivid than anything to be seen even in the most verdant counties of England. The water is clear and glows in the colours of jade, or aquamarine, in accordance with the changes of light. Today we venture ashore. I am reassured by the memory of a conversation I had with Captain Colefax at Portsmouth, who said we might expect a good welcome here, and no hostility, although a very considerable interest and curiosity in our appearance and doings.

September 25 Hallard, the second mate, died during the early hours of this morning, of an abdominal perforation, accompanied by high fever, for which there could be found no relief or remedy. He lay unconscious for some six hours, but at the last was able to hear some comfortable words read to him from the Prayer Book and the New Testament, and died a good death. He was buried at sea, and saluted by the whole ship's company, and there was much sadness, for he was a favourite with many, and I feel his death as a personal loss to me.

We shall approach the Java straits this day week. God give us a continuance of this fair weather.'

He had read through the first book, and was almost at the end of this, and there were more volumes, bound in bottle-green leather and fastened with clasps; he would read of storms and tropical forests and curious buildings, of birds trailing plumage the colour of jewels and bright enamels, of shoals of porpoise following in the wake of the ship and the night sky crammed with stars, he would read every night, as long as his eyes would stay open, and then lie awake, until the pictures in his head dissolved into dreams, he would travel a thousand miles in minutes and never tire, and listen to the sounds of the sea, of eerie winds and strange voices.

And wake in the morning, uncertain of where he was, and all through the days, there would be hopes singing in him, and fears and uncertainty, too, the sense of guilt and secret betrayal. For he did not know, there was no one, no one who could tell him what he might do, whether he was right to wish himself away, on a ship at sea, whether he would even be truly happy. He did not know. He opened the diaries and read, and closed them, and went out, to walk across the ploughed autumn fields, up on to the ridge. And still, downstairs, in this house, the voices, the anger and the cruel desperate words, the crying. He did not understand any of it, or why there could not be quietness and peace.

Ruth, he thought, and at once felt better. Ruth would know, perhaps she was home again, and if he could be with her, in the cottage, none of it would be important any longer, the voices would not pursue him there.

He sat up suddenly and looked out of the window,

he said, if I could live there with Ruth, I should not want to go away, to be in any other country, or even in another house. Well then, why should he not go to her? Who would care? But he was doubtful about how he could bring himself to ask her, and whether she would want him, for he might remind her too much of Ben; and he knew, in truth, that she liked best to be alone. He could get only so close to her, and no nearer.

He lay down again, and in the end slept, and the echo of their voices rose up and fought with one another, so that his dreams were full of tears and disquiet. He was not awake to hear, at last, that the house had settled back for the night into a tense, mutinous silence.

15

"Where else could I go? 'What could I do?'

But it was not a challenge now, Alice did not speak in defiance and pride; it was a cry for help. There had been so many, during the past weeks, she heard the echo of all their voices, their desperate questions, including her own.

'What could I do?'

Alice leaned her head back against the chair, but her body was still tense, she was afraid.

They had been sitting there for hours like this, talking, or in silence, looking at one another, looking away again. Ruth had not known what to say, not because she was shocked, or even still angry that Alice had come here with her troubles. She had only tried to be gentle, and not to pry, to listen, because she knew none of the answers.

But now, she did ask the one question.

'Why should you not marry him?'

'Marry?'

'Rob Foley. It is his child. He ought to marry you. It's only right.'

'No.'

'Why?'

Alice had scarcely done more than mention the name of the farrier, almost as though it was not relevant, or important to her.

Ruth did not know how long she had been seeing him, what was between them.

'He won't marry me. Not that it matters. Why should it?'

'But if you care for him – if he cares for you, and the baby.'

'He doesn't.'

'He said that?'

'He said, "What's it to me, girl? Others have come here with the same tale. Likely as not, others will come." I knew. I hadn't expected anything more.'

'But that is wicked.'

'No. The truth. At least he tells the truth. He never said he cared for me. He didn't pretend.'

'He made love to you.'

'Oh, Ruth! You don't know anything, do you?'

'Perhaps not. I know what's right, between two people.'

'You had Ben.'

'Yes.'

'No one else. Ever?'

'He was the only person I ever wanted.'

'Do you think I don't know that? And that it was the same for him?'

Her voice rose, it was full of envy again, and the old dislike.

'I'm sorry.'

'Why should you be? Ben is dead. You know about that. I know about other things.'

'But what about you? Do you love him?'

Alice was silent for a while, running her forefinger along the edge of the chair. Ruth had lit a fire, the first of the winter, she had carried in the ash logs which Ben had felled and brought home, the week before he died, she had laid them carefully in the grate, the way he had taught her. But setting light to them had startled and pained her, she had felt some kind of guilt, as the first blue flames had begun to lick and coil like snakes' tongues around the logs. For she was burning and destroying one more piece of the past, the old life. And it would vanish into smoke and never come again.

But they sat beside the grate, and the fire warmed them both, and gave them something to look at, when they could not talk, and the smell of the woodsmoke was full of memories.

Alice said, 'I think that I have never loved anyone in my life. Except Ben. Except my brother.'

Ruth felt a shock go through her. But after it, a curious sense of warmth, of understanding and relief. This was why Alice had never liked her, then, had resented her, tried to put her down. This. Love for Ben. And Ruth had taken him away.

But love for Ben was a bond between them, too, the

first there had ever been. And he had had to die before it could reveal itself and be accepted by them.

Now, Alice was expecting a child, by a man she cared nothing for; why had she ever gone with him at all? If there had been no love or even liking, what else could there have been?

'Don't you know what it's like, living in that house? Can't you imagine? How I have hated it, hated them for years. There was only ever Ben to make it feel like a home, a place you could be happy in. Be yourself. Then he was dead and there was nothing. Only my mother, wailing and weeping, and my father – and what use is he to anyone?'

'Jo...'

'Jo? He's a child.'

No, Ruth thought, oh no, for Jo understood more than any of them. But she did not say it.

'And all these years, I've had to sit and listen to her. What she was planning for me, what I was going to be, the chances I was going to have. She's never wanted me to live my life, she wanted me to live hers for her, be the person she chose. She's never known what I am really like. Or any of us. She only cares about herself. She calls me "Proud". Well, what about her? What is running through her all the time but pride? I had to do something, get out, go somewhere. Did it matter where? So long as I was showing her I could find a way of my own.'

'Yes.'

For Ruth saw well enough how things had been, why Alice had gone off, out of frustration and spite, to Rob Foley the farrier, though she did not care twopence for him. He was everything Dora Bryce despised, a man she would not think good enough to give so much as a good-day to any daughter of hers.

So Alice was having a child, and she had been told never to go back to that house in Foss Lane; she might do what she pleased, have her baby or lose it, make her own way as best she might, find friends, a home or a husband, or not. Dora Bryce did not care.

'She went on shouting and screaming. "Get out of here, get out." She wouldn't listen to what he said – he'd have let me stay. He wants a quiet life. "Anything for a quiet life." He's not ashamed of me. But she said, "Get out of this house." And I was glad enough to go, it's not a place I care to stay in for the rest of my life, is it?'

She closed her eyes. Her skin was taut and pale with exhaustion. Ruth thought, how can people be like that, turn their own children out, not even listen or forgive? That is not how anyone should be.

She said, 'I'm glad you thought to come here. It was the right thing.'

'I don't want you to pity me. I don't want you to let me stay here out of duty. Because I am Ben's sister. You needn't think that's any use.'

'No.'

'I'll find somewhere to go. I'll manage. When I can think.'

'You should stay here.'

'You don't like me.'

'I don't know you,' Ruth said, and that was the truth. 'I have never known you.'

'Did you ever want to? Try to?'

'No.'

'You had Ben. You didn't think about anything else at all.'

'No.'

'Oh, I don't blame you for that. You needn't think I blame you.'

She began to cry, then, though quite silently, letting the tears run down and dry on her cheeks, and Ruth only sat on beside her, saying nothing, she spread out her hands to the fire and gazed into it. But she thought, how many tears? Oh God, how many tears have there been? How much unhappiness and despair and exhaustion and anger and loneliness and misunderstanding? For it seemed at this moment that all the people she had ever known in her life had been weeping, all the days and nights of the past months had been full of nothing but tears.

And will it go on like this? Oh, for how much longer will it go on?

*

She made up a bed in the small room, and Alice went to it early, worn out. Ruth sat on by the fire for over an hour, until she was sure that Alice must have gone to sleep. There were no sounds within the house, except for the shifting of the logs, the spurts and sparks of the flames. Yet it felt quite different, another person was here, and her presence seemed to fill every corner of every room.

Ruth knew that what she must do now was as much for herself as for Alice, it was the only possible step, and she was the only person who could take it. She could not stay here, quite alone, not caring for anything else, did not even want that any longer. It was wrong. That was no way to live. Somehow, all the quarrels and unspoken hostilities had to be healed over, and forgotten, and she was as much to blame for them as any one, perhaps more.

She took her coat and went out. The wind was still high now, blowing hard at her from behind, almost lifting her off the ground. The trees were straining and tossing about, like ships caught in a storm. The last, sweet-rotten death-smells of autumn were being driven out, to make way for the first, cold, clear airs of winter. In the woods, the leaves would be falling and piling up in drifts like dry snow, tomorrow, the sky would show in neat patches through the network of bare branches.

There was no moon. But she was used to all these paths and lanes at night, she could have walked through any of the fields or copses and found her way easily, would know every step, even if she had been blind.

At the corner of Foss Lane, she stopped, to get back her breath, and her courage, and half-hoped, now, that they would already have gone to bed, and she would have an excuse to turn back. For she was afraid of them, did not know what she might say, how to begin. They might have been people who spoke another language, so great was the distance between them.

She said, they are the same, they are human beings, have the same feelings and miseries, are lonely, growing older. They are the same. Were they?

There was a light showing behind the closed curtains. She pressed her arms hard against her sides, and began to walk slowly towards the house. She said, 'Help me, please help me.' And it was Ben she was talking to, she was still half-helpless without him, could never be certain if what she did or said was right. '*Help me.*'

The wind came thundering down the narrow street.

Walking into that room, behind Arthur Bryce, she remembered how it had been the first time, with Ben, and how she had felt, and it might have been a hundred years ago, she was so changed. But they were not. Dora Bryce looked at her, without interest. Did not speak.

The room was very hot, a fire banked high up in the grate, the furniture crowded in upon her, and she smelled the airless smell, and saw again those black figures who had perched on all the chairs like crows, staring at her in silent judgment, on the morning of Ben's funeral.

No, she did not blame Alice for wanting to get out of this house, going no matter where.

Arthur Bryce pushed a chair towards her, too close to the fire, but she took it, and sat on the very edge and her throat closed up, her tongue felt swollen and dry. '*Help me.*'

In the end, he spoke, he said, 'There's a wind. A bit of a wind tonight.'

'Yes.' And then went on quickly, looking at Dora Bryce, said, 'I came to tell you about Alice. That she's all right. She's at the cottage. I thought...'

'I won't have her name spoken in this house. I'll thank you not to come here, reminding us, bringing it all up again. It's done with. She's shamed us, and how do you think I feel?'

'Please. Listen ...' Ruth was calm now, she would not be angry. There had been enough of that.

'What have you come here for, all of a sudden?'

'I wanted ... I know I should have come long before. To say I was sorry. I wanted to do something – say something to you.'

'What is there to say?'

'Dora ..?

But she turned and looked at her husband in scorn, and he fell silent again, hunched down further into his chair, easily defeated.

'You've never had time for us.'

'I wanted to change things. To try. And to tell you that Alice can stay with me, you can see her there. If that's what she wants.'

'Yes, you're two of a kind, you've neither of you had any thought for others.'

'That's not ...' But she checked herself at once. 'We should be friends. Oh, where is the point in all this, where will it end? Why should we go on, not liking one another, not seeing one another? Not even trying. At least we can try.'

Dora Bryce only looked away from her again, and at the fire.

Ruth said desperately, 'For Ben. Shouldn't we think of being friends for his sake? He was your son and my husband. We've gone through the same things, haven't we? We've felt the same, because he is dead? Why hasn't that brought us together? It should, it should.'

'How do you know what I've felt. You don't know anything. I carried him, I gave birth to him, I reared him. What can you know about all of that?'

'Nothing. No. But...'

'You none of you know.'

'Others have been hurt,' Arthur Bryce said slowly, 'there's ways of being hurt and other ways. But it's the same in the end.'

Ruth thought of the night he had come up to the churchyard to see the grave-dressing, how there had been a closeness between them then, a sharing of love and grief. There was no bitterness between Arthur Bryce and herself, though they knew one another hardly at all.

'Alice ...'

'Haven't I told you, haven't you heard? She's gone. She's brought it upon herself, and I won't have her spoken of.'

'But she's unhappy. She is frightened.'

'You didn't hear the things she said, to my face, what she called me, here, in this room last night. What have I done to deserve that?'

'Other people have made the same mistake. And she is the one who has to have the baby, on her own. She didn't know what she was saying to you.'

'She knew. And she knows what I said. And I meant it. Every word of it.'

'But you are her mother.'

'I'm not proud of that.'

Ruth wanted to weep at her own helplessness, she felt as though she were battering with her fists and tearing with her fingers at some great, barred and bolted door.

'Won't you ever see her? Won't you help her?'

'I've said all I have to say.'

'And me? What about me? Can't you forgive me, whatever I've done, try to like me... try. . . I was Ben's wife.'

Silence. The fire blazed up. Ruth was faint with the heat, and the effort she had made, and hurt, too, because she had come here, summoned up all her courage, had truly wanted to like, and be liked, and bury what was past, to bring them together, all of them. She had failed. There was nothing more she could do. She did not speak to Dora Bryce again.

The wind was wilder, it was very cold, but she welcomed it, after the heat and anger and tension in that room. Arthur Bryce touched her arm as she opened the gate.

'She's not herself. She's upset. It's hard for her, she'd always hoped such a lot, wanted such a lot for the girl. It's hard.'

'Yes.'

'Don't hold it against her.'

She turned and looked at him. She thought, and he loves her. He still loves her, no matter what she does or says.

'What about you?' she asked him. 'Do you want to see Alice? Have her come home?'

He shook his head. 'She's made her mistake. She'll pay for it. She'll go through enough.'

'And needs people, doesn't she? Needs you and her mother – all of us.'

'In time,' he said, glancing back at the house, 'give it time. It'll settle down. Things do. In time.'

'You know where to come, if you want to see her.'

'You're a good girl, Ruth.' He pressed her arm. 'I was glad for him – Ben. Did I ever say it? You're a good girl.'

She would have replied, told him that things were well between them, at least, but he left her and shambled back to the house, and only half-raised a hand to her, before closing the door.

'Well, I have tried,' she said, 'I have done what I could.' And set off, back through the lanes and out of the village, in the darkness and the wind.

*

Jo lay flat on his stomach on top of the ridge. There had been the wind, and then rain, and all the colours had been washed out of the world and rinsed away. It was dry today, dry and still and clear. The bare fields dropped away and then rose again, and in the far distance they were like a haze of smoke. The sky was milk-white. He looked over to where the beech woods spread out, in ranks and rows like an army of iron-clad soldiers, waiting to move forwards and take over the land. Two magpies went winging away above his head, black and white.

Through the nights of the gales, he had lain awake and felt his bed rising and falling on the wind, had heard the shifting of the trees like the waves of a sea. He had said, I will go away. And dreamed of it.

Now, it was not the same. All that morning, he had been walking through the woods, gone down to where the river ran, gleaming like metal, between its banks. He had listened to the shush of his own footsteps as he waded through the soft piles of dead leaves, had touched the cold bark of ash and larch and beech trees and felt a twig crack under him, brittle as bone. He had stood in Helm Bottom and smelled the frost and fungus and sensed the presence of dozens of sleeping animals in holes and sets and hidden lairs all about him. And then he had come up here, and it was like being on the roof of the world. The sheep calls came to him from far away. There was so much space, now, so much room to breathe. He felt like a god here, able to see so far.

And he knew that he could never go away, could never be happy at sea, in other countries. This was his place, as it had been Ben's, he belonged to the woods and ditches and copses and streams, needed to live among the calls of birds and the ferreting, scratching, rustling of the feet of squirrels and foxes and badgers, in the undergrowth, to smell the wind of winter and the sap of spring and have the heat of the summer sun warm his body.

He would not go. And there were other reasons. There was Ruth, whom he could never leave, and his mother and father, who did not understand him, but who needed him, he could see that in their eyes, because Ben was gone, and now Alice. They could not bear to lose him, too. He knew himself, knew that he was very like Ben, and so, in his own way, must take Ben's place. In a little over a year he would leave school, and then he would go and work for Rydal, train as a forester or a gamekeeper.

He turned over on to his back and looked up at the wide, pale sky. He closed his eyes, and felt the earth as it turned, and was rocked by it.

*

The year moved to its end, and the countryside settled down into winter, the bracken and grass on the common were shrunken and dark. Some remembered, others forgot, the death of Ben Bryce. But they were all changed, in some way, the year had brushed against them all, as it passed.

Ratheman's wife was taken to a hospital miles away, and her baby sent to be cared for by her sister, and Ratheman himself stayed on alone in the dark house, and prayed and wept, and thought, sometimes, of Ruth Bryce; and when he did so, it seemed to him that he might be able to bear it all, to accept and come through. Though he lay awake every night, and then he felt far away from any human being, and out of the reach of God, far from understanding any truth, or of receiving any hope or consolation. The nights went on forever but he could not face the day either, when it did, at last, come seeping through the curtains.

Alice Bryce would not go out, but people heard about her, just the same, and talked, and Rob Foley had another girl, Annie Peters, who worked at Rydal's and went to the farrier's house on Sundays, and thought that she loved him. People went on, worked, prepared for the hardness of winter, and out in his tin hut, old Moony died, one November night, and the raven sat silent, huddled into its feathers, looking at the man's body under its blanket, and it was three weeks before he was found, by Potter, who had come out here, walking his dog. Potter looked down again, at death, and shook his head, for this time, it was a cold, lonely, comfortless thing, and who had ever bothered about old Moony?

In the house in Foss Lane, Dora Bryce would not speak of her daughter, but she thought, sitting by the hot fire every evening, felt the beginnings of interest in the unborn child. At night, sensing that she lay awake, and remembering the griefs and losses of that year, Arthur Bryce put his injured arm about her, and wished that he were a different man, so that she might gain more strength from him. Upstairs, Jo let down the lid of his great-grandfather's trunk quietly, and tied up the straps and pushed it into the far corner of his room, behind a curtain, before he went to bed and slept.

The first ice and a hard frost came, and the water was solid in tanks and sinks, and hung down like stalactites from the taps in the yard at Rydal's farm. But there was not yet any snow. At night, the sheep ran down to the bottom of the fields, and huddled together and their bodies were heavy and shapeless under the thick, matted fleece.

December came. It was Sunday. Ruth went out of the back door, and walked half way down the garden, to stand, just between the apple trees, in the place she had been that afternoon, when she had felt the shock at the moment of Ben's death. Her breath smoked on the steel-cold night air, and the grass and the vegetable tops were coated with a thin frost, like powdered sugar.

She was quite alone. But not alone. She was the same person, Ruth Bryce. But not the same. She loved Ben, and wanted him, and still did not know how she might live for the rest of her life. But Ben was dead, and laid in his grave, and she would move on, from one day to the next. There was winter. There would be spring.

In her bed in the small room, Alice slept, her legs curled up and her arms resting on her rounded belly. Ruth did not know how she felt, what she thought, and perhaps they would never truly like one another, never be close. But for the time being, grief and trouble and the memory of Ben had drawn them together, they got on, well enough, passed the days, while Alice waited for the birth of her child. Jo came to see them. And once, Arthur Bryce had come, and though he had said little enough, Ruth was glad, for Alice's sake and for her own. For she had heard about old Moony, and felt appalled, at the isolated death, that the man had

had no friends, no care. She must not let anyone in her own life come to that.

She let her hand slide down the tree trunk, and fall to her side, and shivered. And walked up the path to the house, which was no longer empty, no longer hers alone. She said, 'Ben,' once, cried out the name.

As she turned, in the doorway, she saw a fox slip down the garden, silent, purposeful. But the hens were locked away, safe, and the fox passed on, down through the meadow towards the dark woods.

The donkey Balaam stood, still as a statue, grey as granite, under the riding moon.

Ruth closed the door.

www.vintage-books.co.uk